Angels
In The Snow

*May all who read these pages first grow
tender hearts to weep for these precious little
martyrs and then grow fiercely brave hearts
to stand up and fight for them!*

God bless you.

~Heath Christopher Goodman

Sandra Lee Weaver
June 22nd, 1939 - December 20th, 2002
Loving mother, wife, sister, friend and child of God

This book is dedicated to my precious mother now in the bosom of the Heavenly Father's care. She was the one when I was a little boy who would warm my frost bitten fingers when I came crying into the house from playing too long out in the Indiana winter cold. Because of my birth defects, I don't have great circulation in my fingers. She would lovingly scold me for not wearing my mittens and for not coming in from the cold sooner. Then she would delicately rub my little fingers until they were warmed up and no longer hurting.

However, she did this not only with my little boy hands but also with my little boy heart. Many times it was my mother's unconditional love and care that sheltered me from the icy, harsh rejection that I received from those who ridiculed and snubbed me for my birth defects.

Yes, the winter of my childhood was sometimes cruel and cold but I thank God for my precious Mama... my angel in the snow.

Angels In The Snow

It's time to come in from the cold.

HEATH CHRISTOPHER GOODMAN

CREATIVE
WORKS
PRESS

Leave Your Mark On The World.

ISBN: 978-1-951965-00-6 (Paperback)
Kindle Edition Available Through Amazon

Library of Congress Control Number: 2019919920

Any references to historical events, real people, or real places are used fictitiously. Names, characters, and places are products of the author's imagination.

Book design by CreatorGraphics.com

First printing edition 2019.

Creative Works Press
2001 Duncan Dr. NW Ste. #44
Kennesaw, GA 30156
404-307-9185
sales@creatorgraphics.com

www.CreativeWorks.cloud
www.CreatorGraphics.com

Book/Ministry Websites:
www.AngelsInTheSnow.net
www.SavePreciousBabies.com

Preface

Then I saw little babies as far as the eye could see, cradled in the arms of a great army of towering angels who had laid down their swords to care for them. Satan had desired to sift them like wheat. Heaven had taken them in when they were rejected by the world.

Precious little ones, beautiful, beautiful babies! There were so many of them. I told the angel who showed me these things, "Pity these children who missed out on earth!" But the angel gently shook his head no and said, "Pity the world who missed out on Heaven!"

"But Jesus sent for them, saying, Let the children come to me, and do not keep them away, for of such is the kingdom of heaven."
Luke 18:16

The End

The sunshine was in mourning that morning, hiding her face as only a subtle light infused the thick grey clouds. The low sky created a sense of dreariness upon the snowy, cold, landscape outside of rural Bloomington, home of Indiana University. Several police cars with their lights flashing were parked near a snow embankment adjacent to a recently renovated farmhouse. There was also an ambulance with it's lights flashing, as well as another unmarked police vehicle nearby. Police crime scene tape had been put up around the homestead to keep curious, nosy neighbors from contaminating the tragic scene.

The frozen corpse of a strikingly beautiful young woman, identified as Jenny Abernathy in her late twenties was lying on a nearby hillside. Her body, lightly covered in the snow and frost from the previous night's flash arctic front. She had apparently died from hypothermia brought on by an extreme temperature drop due to the bitter storm that had quickly come and gone. Only a residual howling wind and biting cold remained.

Detective Cameron, a scruffy bearded gentleman with untrendy glasses bundled up in a thick Parka was blankly staring in the general vicinity of where the body laid. EMS personnel were working to remove the corpse. As a weary veteran of the Ellettsville police department,

Detective Cameron, shook his head nonchalantly as he took a sip of his convenient store coffee. He was just thinking about how tired and weary he was of seeing such tragedy, such sad circumstantial cases.

The harsh cold wind intermittently blew on his exposed head, stinging his ears. He looked over at his newbie partner, Detective Scott Garvin, early 30's, also well bundled up.

Detective Garvin had just downloaded the police scene photos he had taken with his phone onto a laptop sitting on the hood of their patrol car. Detective Cameron took over the laptop as he ran a forensic A.I. software program to analyze the photos and notes. Detective Garvin broke the silence between him and his superior. "Did you see all the pictures in her home office of her with all those high profile politicians and celebrities, Boss? What do you think that's all about? She looks like she could have been a celebrity herself, so very pretty."

Detective Cameron blinked lethargically. "Yes, I saw them. She was a big star here at IU and a leading political advocate in the woman's movement. Lot's of friends in high places, I guess... such a shame... So anyways, tell me whatcha've got Sherlock?" Detective Cameron broke his gaze away from the corpse and fixed his eyes on his partner.

"This one's almost definitely a suicide, cut and dry, no weird bullets or bones to be found here, I think... am I right, Boss?" Detective Garvin smugly replied. Their breath could be seen in the air, in the backdrop of the dismal lights flashing on the winter landscape.

Detective Cameron mused a bit. "Okay, Scotty Boy, do please tell me why you are making this grand assumption so quickly and forthright. You've ruled out foul play altogether... so please let me in on your lickety split, open and shut deductions here."

"Well, for starters... apparently our victim has a history of some mental problems, mild psychosis, suicidal threats made before... and extreme depression. We found an old prescription bottle recently emptied on her bathroom floor. There's only one set of foot prints out here, clearly coming from the house. She wandered out here and plopped herself down to die intentionally... or maybe accidentally on purpose, not sure which..." Detective Garvin looked at his partner for signs of affirmation but he clearly refrained from giving any.

Detective Cameron just stared expressionless at the now covered corpse. He looked cold, totally frozen in thought. Detective Garvin then continued voicing his thoughts where he had left off. "Triggered and emotionally distraught by something, she clearly trashed her house, took whatever amount of pills was in that bottle... and I am assuming the autopsy will show an elevated dosage in her blood... which surely helped speed up the process of her inability to fight her greater instinct to survive and perhaps also helped in causing her to freeze to death much sooner."

"But as she made her way out here last night, for some odd reason, not being in her right mind, she evidently made this here snow angel impression... or perhaps it was some sort of freakish, drug induced struggle in the snow... where she continued to lay here until unconscious, her body finally succumbing to hypothermia and the harsh cold elements. Tada, not rocket science... or I don't think Alfred Hitchcock murder mystery type stuff going on here Boss..."

Detective Garvin again looked up to get affirmation from his veteran partner who still looked as frozen as the corpse he was watching being put in the ambulance.

Detective Cameron finally blinked to show he really was among the living. "You might be right Scotty but never completely rule out that this scene could be staged to look like a suicide... It looks pretty good on the surface of the initial circumstantial and forensic evidence. And you know, I know there are a lot of dumb criminals out there, but believe it or not, there are some that have half a brain to make a murder look like something else. You know, hashtag Jeffrey Epstien didn't kill himself."

Detective Cameron continued. "Because she's such a high profile political activist for abortion and women's rights... who knows maybe some Bible thumping, fanatical Christian whacked her and staged her suicide... maybe some church or right-wing religious organization put a hit on her... you know, the world is full of unhinged religious folks these days." Detective Cameron smirkingly looked over at his partner to see his reaction.

"You're not serious, are you Boss? I mean, yea, there could be a Bible toting, radicalized extremist out there but highly doubtful in this case. Every political side has fringe anomalies but we can't stereotype a whole group of people like Christians just because of a few bad apples. The greater population of peace loving church folks who hold the belief that abortion is murder are not really suspect to commit the very crime they protest." Detective Gavin let out a sarcastic laugh and continued. "It goes against their basic morals, logic and the fundamental tenets of their faith... but yea, I guess in these more turbulent times... I'm sure there may be some unhinged religious nuts that could do it."

Detective Cameron mused with intrigue at his partner's answer, shook his head. "Scotty Boy, I'm just yanking your chain a little here. I know you are a church going, family man yourself... but sometimes you do have to think outside your own paradigm. We're not living in apple pie, Leave-It-To-Beaver Americana anymore."

Detective Garvin nodded his head in agreement. "Yes, you are right, Boss, but in this case, I don't see a political conspiracy thriller... but more like a sad, sad tragedy. Of course, this is just my preliminary conjecture, right? Not set in stone yet. I know we need to follow up and double down on looking for anything out of sync with this initial take. But at this point, in my gut, Boss, I don't have any red flags being set off, as this being any more than a sad, lonely woman who finally ended what she thought was a miserable existence. Tell me, what does your gut really say, Boss?"

Detective Cameron noticeably shuttered in his countenance as he listened to the last of his partner's remarks. "Yes, I'm afraid you're hitting the marks. It doesn't look out of the ordinary to me either... which is actually ironic and sad to say. What a tragic thing really, for such a pretty young woman who has so much to live for... to end her life like this. Nice house, nice car, luxurious lifestyle... prestige and notoriety, the whole world at her fingertips. What would cause someone to end their life like this? It just doesn't add up."

Detective Gavin answered back, who was also in a reflective pose. "Well, you know as well as I do, money and all these things are superficial distractions in our lives... None of them are worth living for or dying for, really... It's people, our relationships, human interaction, or lack of it, that make us or break us."

Both detectives reflected and watched as the ambulance started to back out slowly and head down the road. Detective Cameron looked back one last time where the body once laid. He shook his head. "I don't know what her last thoughts were in the freezing dead of night with a blizzard raging around her... as she deliberately fell there and made that novel, playful impression in the snow... like some happy child would make..." He paused with visible sympathy, frowning, shaking his head in disapproval as they both made their way to the unmarked patrol car. Detective Cameron then continued just as they reached the car door. "But clearly Scotty Boy, whatever was going on out here last night with this poor Ms. Jenny girl, she had no snow angels watching over her!"

The two detectives glanced somberly across the top of the patrol car at each other before entering the vehicle. They drove off leaving only a few police cars and sheriff's spokespersons at the scene with some local news crews arriving to make their broadcast.

The yellow police tape flapped in the early morning wind. Grey clouds continued to hover low as police lights bounced off them making a melancholic scene for the journalists. Who would have known that just moments before, the corpse of the beautiful Jenny Abernathy laid sadly and mysteriously frozen in a now unrecognizable, angelic snowy imprint?

The Family

A fresh snow covered the southern Indiana landscape. Nestled within a large array of pine trees, a country home with a wrap around porch bellowed out smoke from its chimney-stack. It was an older farmhouse with faded paint and exposed wood. There were a few Christmas ornaments and lights sprawled around the house in an attempt to brighten the aged and well worn look. An older, blue minivan was parked in the front driveway.

The day was slowly winding down with low, thick clouds that seemed to shout "More snow to come!" The air was slightly nippy but nothing uncommon or unbearable to the rural residents of Ellettsville, a town not far from Bloomington, home of the Hoosiers and Indiana University.

Jenny Daniels was hiding with her six year old daughter Kaley on the side of a snowy embankment in the back area of their home. They both were overly dressed for a blizzard. Jenny was almost thirty. She was a beautiful Caucasian with long coal black hair and the most stunning blue eyes. Her daughter was truly a carbon copy of her.

Jenny and Kaley crouched low with both their hearts beating fast with adrenaline. Jenny had her mitten draped, pointing a finger up to her lips as she looked intensely at her daughter. "Hush Kaley,

Shhhhhhhhh. Don't let them hear you. Come closer to the snow pile. I think they're coming around from the other side of the house. Shush!"

Kaley giggled and obeyed. She scooted close to her mother. "I'm trying Mommy but it's so funny. Where are they? I don't see them! They must be hiding from us too." They both crouched as low as they could and tried to be as silent as possible, their hearts still beating a mile a minute. The sound of hurried footsteps crunching the snow soon grew louder as Jenny and Kaley froze every muscle in their bodies to stay as quiet as they could. There was a shout and then the footsteps grew even closer. Jenny could tell her daughter was faltering. She pressed her finger up to her lips again. "Shshshsh." But Kaley couldn't hold the suspense any longer. She soon burst out with the loudest giggle ever. Their cover was blown.

Jenny knew it was now fight or flight as the footsteps were now on top of them. She made a fresh snowball and told her daughter to do the same. From around the corner of the white embankment came two other winter draped figures. One, Travis, was tall and built like a train, the other, Kenny was short, and more like a cute caboose.

Kenny wore a warm aviator hat that had two goggles designed on it. They both had a snowball in each hand and prepared to do battle with their archenemies. The little one was the first to fire. A snowball barely hit Jenny in the shoulder and then another hit Kaley's foot as it was launched prematurely. Jenny and Kaley fired back at Kenny, Kaley's twin brother. He too was an echo image of his mother, save the boyish features of his father.

Kenny was hit hard as incoming snowballs pelted his upper torso and the forehead of his aviator hat. The bigger fellow in a brown snow cap that covered all of his ears was also now on the scene. Travis was Jenny's beloved husband and the father of her twins. He fired his snowballs at the hiding menaces, trying to give his sidekick time to reload.

Kenny reloaded and fired. Now snowballs flew in all directions and a frosty Armageddon ensued. Even their snowman, Frostypants, a recently created snow being in the center of the front yard became a victim. He was used as a human shield against incoming white bombs. Screams and laughter sounded across the snowy landscape.

"Missed me, missed me, now you got to kiss me!" Travis teased as he dodged Jenny's snowballs. Jenny laughed so heartily as Travis was distracted with her and was pelted by Kaley from the other side. Kaley managed to plant one near the center of his chest.

As the Daniels family grew tired of the snow wars, they would soon all collapse in front of the now wounded snowman, Frostypants. Kaley and Kenny sparked on about various triumphant moments of the snow battles as mom and dad corrected versions of half truths and exaggerations.

The Daniels were a beautiful family that had truly gone through some tough times. Even though they didn't have much, they compensated for it by having each other. Yes, the little home they lived in was a bit rickety and raggedy but it was a blessing anyways. It was an inherited gift from Jenny's grandmother, affectionately called "Grannygrans". They didn't have a mortgage which really helped a lot. Especially since they were in the final year of paying back both Travis's and Jenny's huge student loans. Travis reflected on this as he sat leaned up against Frostypants. "Soon we'll have some funds to be able to start fixing up this ol' place." His mind wandered from his family's wacky conversation.

"Only five more days till Christmas!" Kaley suddenly exclaimed.

"Yea, then we can open our presents! Daddy, are you going to open the one from me first?" Kenny asked.

"Well, I might just do that, Scout. We'll see."

"Last year I got the best Christmas gift ever remember? I got the electric train set!" Kenny sparked. "My best Christmas gift ever was all my little ponies." Kaley inserted.

"What was your best Christmas gift ever, Daddy?" Kenny turned to Travis who was currently doing reconstructive cosmetic surgery on Frostypants.

"My best Christmas gift ever... hmmm. That's a tough one. Maybe the exercise equipment that I got from Mommy, you and Kaley last year."

"What about you, Mommy? What is the best Christmas gift you ever got?" Kaley made sure her mommy wasn't left out of their little holiday survey.

"Hmmm. Well that is really a hard one for me to answer too. I'll have to think about that. All my gifts have been so wonderful!" Jenny beamed.

"Yea, me too." Kaley added.

"Well, how about going in and warming up to the fire now with a cup of hot cocoa?" Jenny asked as she discerned all her cold, wet and weary soldiers.

"Yea, and with marshmallows and whipped cream too!" Kenny blasted. His hat was now folded up to his head to reveal his frosty cheeks and runny nose.

"That sounds like a great idea!" Travis inserted.

"I get the Snoopy mug!" Kaley blurted out to be relevant with the new plan.

Almost in unison, the Daniels family stood up to go inside. A fresh snow began to fall again.

"Wait, Mommy, we forgot to do something important!" Kaley spoke up as everyone turned towards the front porch.

"What?" Jenny looked at her smiling daughter who was truly a bright spot in her world. "We forgot to make our snow angel family!" Kaley grabbed her mother's hand. "Oh yea." Both Travis and Jenny answered back.

It had become a tradition with Kaley and Kenny for the last few years to make angels in the snow with mom and dad plopped on either side to make it an official "snow angel family".

"Let's do it where we did it before on the side of the hill in the front yard between Mr. and Mrs. Apple Tree and the road." Kenny piped up.

"Yes, that seems to be the family tradition." Travis said, mimicking an old person's voice as he ruffled the aviator hat on his son's head.

The four of them shuffled to the side of their front yard where two Gala apple trees grew on top of a hilly slope. All the first fruits of the apple trees were already gone and there were no leaves. Just frosted, snow covered branches.

The little family each got into position, about an arm's length away from one another. They all plopped to the ground and flapped their arms and legs. They also tried to catch snowflakes with their tongues as they lay spread out in the snow.

A car full of onlookers passed slowly by as the Daniels flapped in the snow. Travis and Jenny began to laugh as they thought how funny they must look to the folks going by.

"We probably won't be getting any Christmas cards from our neighbors this year!" Travis poked fun as he looked at his wife. Jenny laughed and was the first to get up to view her angel. Travis, Kaley and Kenny followed and soon the four of them were looking down at their angel creations.

"See Mom, the angels will protect our family and home from every side, just like Daddy prays at night, one for the north, one for the south, one for the west and one for the east!" Kaley cited as they peered down.

"Exactly, my love, that's right! Okay, let's march our cold tushes in the house and make some of Grannygran's hot chocolate!" Jenny exclaimed.

"Yea, I'm freezing now!" Kenny shivered out loud.

"I'm all in for that!" Travis beamed as he picked Kenny up into his arm and put his hand around Jenny. Kaley walked beside them as they all four tromped to the front porch.

The Seeds

Inside the little rickety humble home, a pleasant aroma of milk chocolate saturated the senses. The home was filled with little shelves with various knickknacks of anything country or rustic. For a home that lacked the splendor of anything new or shiny, Jenny had made the inside of her home such a cozy, comfortable place to live. The aged wood and faded paint could only be complimented with a rustic theme. Anything else would surely look out of place.

Jenny liked to make the old fashioned hot chocolate her grandmother used to make for her. She had spent many cold winter nights snuggled up to her grandparents in this very house she now lived in. The smell of hot chocolate, the crackling fire warming the living room and the windows frosted over seemed to complete the nostalgic moment.

Travis and the kids were already huddled in the living room, thawing out when she announced that piping hot cocoa was now being served. In the living room the fire place roared with dancing flames that seemed to resonate with quiet joy. A modest Christmas tree with a few gifts underneath it lit up the corner of the room. Above the mantle, a huge picture frame hung with a touching photo of the twins when they were only a few months old. Jenny had given them a sponge bath and had covered them up just a light piece of cloth when they fell asleep. The picture was a Kodak moment of them cuddled so close together. Kaley and Kenny had their arms around the other in a beautiful expression of sibling love. It was so perfect that many assumed that it was somehow a staged moment but Jenny and Travis knew better. It was a totally natural pose and captured the real essence of Kaley's and Kenny's extraordinary bond as they grew older.

The four of them sipped on the whipped cream, marshmallow topped mugs as they made small talk. They watched the fire waltz with the Christmas instrumental music that Travis had inserted into living room's CD player. Kaley, the creative doodler was now spread out on the carpet drawing a picture of the nativity scene with the colored pencils and paper she had gotten from her room.

Kenny was sipping his mug with his toes reaching for the warmth next to his Daddy's in an effort to be like him in every way. "Thank you Mama, this is so wonderful." Travis said as he sipped.

"Yea Mama, thanks for the marshmallows too!" Kenny quipped.

"No problem. It's my treat for my band of snow warriors."

"That was so much fun, we gotta do that again!" Kenny sparked.

Kaley was meticulously coloring without looking up.

"Yes, we do, but next time we ll have to mix it up a little and it will be Kaley and me against you and Mommy." Travis said to his son. Kaley looked up. "Yea, me and Daddy against Scout and Mommy. I think that would be fun too." Kaley called her brother "Scout", a term of endearment for Kenny, mostly used by Travis and Kaley.

"Yea, me and Mommy will be a good team. We both are left-handed and have the same temper... ah... mints!" Kenny inserted, not knowing fully what he was saying. He was trying to repeat one of his daddy's previous conversation about Jenny and Kenny's reactions and "temperaments". Both Jenny and Travis snickered to each other at their son's reaching remark.

"So what are you drawing there, Kaley?" Travis said as he noticed Kaley's undistracted moment.

"It's a picture of when baby Jesus was born in a manger." Kaley swooped up to show her father. "Wow, that's beautiful Kaley. I like the colors. They are so Christmassy. What's that, Christmas trees?" Travis pointed to what looked like two funny shaped Christmas trees that had red dots all over them. "Oh Daddy, you're so silly! That's our new baby apple trees, mine and Scouts from Mr. & Mrs. Apple Tree!"

"Apple trees at the nativity scene? That's nice." Travis winked at his wife who smiled after him.

Kaley suddenly stopped and looked intently at Jenny. "Mommy! Let's go to the laundry room and see if our apple seeds are growing!" Jenny had started a craft project with Kenny and Kaley. They had both planted an apple seed from the two Gala apple trees in the front yard. Kaley and Kenny had playfully named them "Mr. & Mrs. Apple Tree" a year or so before. They germinated the new seeds in separate potted containers and put them in the laundry room next to the window.

"Okay. Let's go and see." Jenny smiled at her daughter's great enthusiasm.

Both Kenny and Kaley raced into the laundry room with Jenny following behind them.

Travis just sat on the couch sipping on his cocoa staring at the fire.

When they arrived, Kaley started jumping up and down in excitement. "Mommy, look! My apple seed is growing. See the little green sprout there!" She pointed inside the pot.

"I see it. That's so wonderful! Jenny said.

Kenny just stared sadly at his pot. "What about your's Kenny? Jenny asked, discerning Kenny's sadness.

"I don't have a green sprout. I don't have any sprout." Kenny's bottom lip stuck out with a whimper.

"Huh, well you just wait, it'll come out like your sister's. Sometimes one seed will grow faster than another, that's all." Jenny spoke trying to comfort him.

"But what if my seed isn't in there? Kenny asked.

"No, your seed is in there, remember when we planted it?" Jenny assured.

"But what if I took it out, Mama? Kenny asked as both a pouting question and an open confession.

"What do you mean, 'took it out', my love?" Jenny caressed her son.

"Well, the other day I came to see if it was growing and it wasn't... so I dug until I found my seed and I took it out to see it better." Kenny confessed all.

"Did you put it back?" Jenny asked.

"I took the seed... to my bedroom... and played with it... a little bit." Kenny was struggling to remember his actions.

"You're not suppose to take it out of the dirt, Kenny, the seed will die!" Kaley loudly and grimly spoke.

"I was going to put it back but it was already dead anyways."

"Oh Kenny, a seed isn't ever really dead. It's only dormant or asleep and once you put in the soil, you have to leave it there so that it can properly grow... to grow up into a mighty apple tree!" Jenny explained.

"But Mama when does the apple seed come alive? Cause it looked like it was very dead to me." Kenny responded.

"When a seed starts to grow, it is alive already. Only living things can really grow, my love and sometimes you can't see it growing right away. An apple seed is really just an apple tree in waiting. So you have to be patient and wait with it." Jenny sang song.

"Yea and like you said last time Mommy, one apple seed today could become an apple orchard tomorrow!" Kaley recited, remembering the first lesson her mother gave on the subject.

Kenny continued to peer down sadly at his pot.

"Yes, my love, but don't you worry Kenny, we will find your apple seed and plant it again. It'll grow. You'll see!" Jenny patted her son's head. "Okay Mama." Kenny sighed.

"For now, we can share this apple tree, Scout." Kaley comforted her brother and handed him her pot. "Yes, that is so sweet of your sister and it's a great idea." Jenny marveled at how loving her daughter could be.

Later that evening as the sun had said "goodbye" and the tired eyes had set in, Jenny was making her rounds to tuck her children into bed. She had already tucked in Kenny and just said "good night" to Kaley and was making her way to her own room. She noticed Kenny's light was on again. She heard him rustling around. She opened the door to his room to find him on the carpet looking for something.

"Kenny, what are you doing, my love?"

Kenny looked up with tears in his eyes. "I'm looking for my apple seed, Mama. I didn't want to kill it. I don't want it to die!"

"Oh honey!" Jenny grabbed her little sad boy and put his head to her chest. "It's okay, my love. You didn't kill it! We'll look for your apple seed tomorrow and it won't die, I promise my love. We'll find your apple seed and give him a second chance! How about that? Your apple seed will live!" She kissed his face.

"You promise?" Kenny's eyes brightened.

"I promise! Now, let's have sweet dreams until the morning!" Jenny re-tucked her son into bed and slipped out quietly to her own room where Travis was already fast asleep.

Jenny lay in her bed thinking about Kenny's sensitive disposition. He was such a tender boy and Travis was right. She could see that he really had her temperament. Jenny loved both her children so very much. As twins they were so alike in their physical features but in their spiritual and social dispositions they were so very different. Kaley seemed more like Travis even though Kenny wanted to be just like him. Kaley was the thinker, and yet the creative one. Kenny was the feeler and yet methodical.

As Jenny lay there, beside Travis, she whispered a prayer of thanks to God for her wonderful little family and their life in her grandmother's home. "Lord, thank you for my little precious family. My Travis, my Kaley, my Kenny. You have blessed me beyond what I could ever have imagined for my life. I am so happy you helped me make the right choices for this simple life I'm living. I wouldn't change it for anything in the whole world..."

Jenny was happy that she made the right decisions that got her to this place in her life. As she began to fade, she snuggled up against Travis. She smelled his peculiar scent. She loved him so much too. He was truly the one that helped her see the light about so many, so many things.

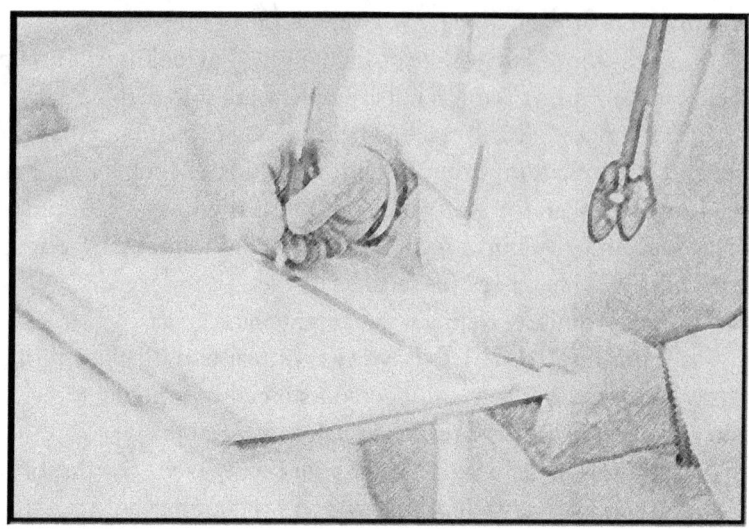

The Procedures

Jenny's eyes were darkened and a blur. She began to focus on the room around her. It looked like a surgical hospital room of some sort. It was immaculate. There were surgical instruments on a table nearby. She tried to get up out of bed but realized she was strapped down to a gurney stretcher. Jenny felt a sharp pain in her abdomen. She was bewildered. Where was she? Why was she strapped down and why was she in a hospital clinic?

Jenny heard a noise to her left. She turned her head to see her son Kenny also strapped down to a stretcher, struggling to get free. "Mama, what's going on here? Why am I like this? Are they gonna kill us, Mama?" Kenny asked.

"Mommy! What are we doing in here?" Jenny heard her daughter Kaley. She turned her head to the right side of her and saw Kaley strapped down to a stretcher also. Kaley was crying very profusely. Jenny tried in vain to get free from the table straps.

"Are you hurt, my love, are you hurt?" Jenny felt a gut wrenching pain in her soul.

"Mommy, why are we here? Why did you bring us to this place?" Kaley spoke through her tears.

"I didn't bring us here. I don't know why we are here, my love!"

"But you did bring us here, Mama." Kenny now cried out from her left.

Jenny turned to see Kenny still struggling to break free. He too started to cry. Jenny struggled also and tried to calm her children.

"I don't know why we are here or what they plan on doing... but I will get to the bottom of this! Don't you worry my loves, I'll get us out of this. Jesus help us! Angels of God help us!" Jenny shouted.

Just then a door opened up and a doctor in a full white medical jacket approached Jenny with a clipboard. "And how is our little patient doing?" The doctor asked.

"Doctor, I am so glad you are here. There's been some sort of mistake. I don't know why I am here or why my children are here but we are okay. We are healthy. We would like to get out of here now!"

The doctor chuckled. "Oh Jenny, you know why you are here! It's time to perform the procedures. It won't take long or inconvenience you too much, I promise. It won't hurt you. Both procedures are very safe, the best care and medical tech in the world. You'll see..."

"What procedures? I don't know anything about any procedures!

The doctor smiled. "Jenny, we have already been over this with you but if you need a refresher, there's a video presentation for you to watch as we actually do the procedure." The doctor instructed the nurse to roll out a cart with a computer monitor on it. The cart was placed between Jenny's stretcher and Kaley's stretcher. Although Jenny could still see Kaley's face, the rest of her was obstructed by the computer monitor.

"Now, we have already given you medicine for sedation and a local anesthetic. This first trimester surgical termination procedure is called Vacuum Aspiration. We use a speculum and dilators to open up your cervix. We will then place a suction catheter to remove the fetal tissue and embryonic fluids." The doctor said matter of factly.

Jenny's eyes widened in horror. "What are you talking about doctor? I don't want this procedure done. I want to leave here immediately with my children!" Jenny screamed as she struggled in the straps.

"Now, now Mrs. Daniels, calm down. You will be fine. The nurse is just now ready with the suction catheter."

Jenny looked over to see a nurse move to her right towards Kaley's stretcher. She had a giant suction tube machine which she positioned onto Kaley. Jenny was frozen in sheer terror. Kaley was struggling, gasping and crying.

"Mommy what are you doing to me? Why do they have this machine attached to me? I want to go home with you and Scout! Don't let them do this to me!"

Jenny burst out with hysterical screaming and crying, struggling as furiously as she could to break free from her straps. Kenny too looked on in horror at what he could see of her sister's face and the computer monitor imagery.

"Kaley, my sister! Kaley, please help her. She's my sister and I love her. Don't hurt her please!" Kenny pleaded with the doctor and nurse. Kaley then looked beyond her own horror to see the tears of her mother and brother. She spoke as if she knew it was the last words she would ever say. "Scout, I love you too. Mama, I love you too. I just want you to know that I forgive you for this Mama... for you know not what you do."

The doctor and nurse completely ignored Jenny, Kaley and Kenny's pleadings for help. They turned on the medical machine. A whirling suction sound could be heard growing louder and louder. The doctor positioned the tip of the suction near Kaley's feet. Kaley looked at her mother and brother one last time and then let out a dying shrill. The computer monitor with a video graphic demonstration displayed in real-time a baby's feet and legs being sucked up into the suction catheter. Kaley screamed in corresponding horror. Then quickly the monitor showed the arms, torso and the head following. The graphic video baby was now completely gone. Kaley was also gone. There was only silence except for the sound of the suction catheter whirling down. The monitor was moved from out of view.

Jenny and Kenny looked towards Kaley's empty stretcher.

"All done doctor! All fetal tissue has been retrieved and accounted for!" The nurse spoke as if it were a simple set of tasks like cleaning an office.

"Good job nurse!" The doctor winked at the nurse and turned to look at Jenny who was completely devastated.

"See Mrs. Daniels, it wasn't that terrible now was it? We'll have you out of here in no time for our next patient. But first we have to do one last procedure. It seems we've made a mistake and you have another baby we have to terminate."

Jenny could hardly speak as she was in so much disbelief and shock. Kenny continued to struggle and cry on his stretcher.

Jenny shouted despairingly at the doctor. "You've killed my daughter! My precious daughter! How could you?" Jenny then remembered her son and turned to see him so gripped with grief and fear. "Kenny, I love you baby. I won't let them do that to you!"

"No, Jenny because the fetus is much more developed now and actually much more viable than your daughter. We will have to do 3rd trimester surgical procedures. One is called an Induction and the other is called a D&E. But don't you worry. Even though it's a little more risky and complicated, we have an excellent record of success. It's perfectly fine really. We do these procedures every day, 10 times a day or more!" The doctor spoke as if he were about to perform a life saving operation on her.

Jenny raged against the doctor. "I didn't want your first procedure and I don't want these either! Listen to me, I want to go home with my son! Don't you understand? Please doctor! I want to keep my babies!"

Kenny burst out with fear. "Am I going to die like Kaley, Mama? I don't want to die Mama. You promised me I would live. Give me a second chance, Mama. Am I really just a mass of tissue that anyone can just throw away? Don't I have a right to live, Mama!"

Jenny struggled and cried to contain herself. "Yes, you do, my love. Please hold on. Hold on, my son!" She turned again to the doctor. "Please doctor uphold your Hippocratic oath and save lives, don't kill them!" Both the doctor and nurse ignored her outburst as they continued prepping for the procedure. The doctor stuck Jenny with a big syringe in her abdomen region. They then moved the computer monitor between Jenny and Kenny as they did with Kaley. Jenny could only see Kenny's head and shoulders. The computer monitor showed a graphic in real-time of an injection being given in the abdomen, piercing the lining of the womb and the syringe going into the head of the graphic video baby.

"We've just given you a Digoxin injection. This will cause fetal demise normally within a short amount of time."

Kenny suddenly screamed with horrifying shrieks. He struggled violently on the stretcher. "Aaahhh. Mama! My head hurts real bad now. I feel pain all over my body! What's happening to me? Mama, why did you do this to me? I thought I was your baby boy?" He began to choke and his hands broke loose from the straps to grasp his head. "I can hardly breathe Mama!"

Jenny stared helplessly at her son in excruciating pain. "Oh no, no my love. Kenny, I love you so much! You ARE my baby boy! I don't know why they are doing this to us! Breathe, baby breath for Mama please!" Jenny turned back to the doctor. "For God's sake do something doctor, you are suppose to heal people not hurt them!"

Her anger turned to the most humble plea. "Please doctor... please don't do this to my baby."

The doctor looked annoyed. "Calm down, Mrs Daniels, the procedure is almost complete. It won't be long now!"

The doctor then watched Kenny struggling less but still very much alive. He instructed the nurse to prepare another Digoxin injection which showed up in real-time as a graphic on the computer monitor as well. "Nurse, we're going to have to inject more Digoxin. The fetus is still alive and struggling."

"Yes doctor. Should I gather the D&E instruments also?"

"Sure, be prepared now for this too." The doctor injected more Digoxin in Jenny's abdomen.

Jenny continued to plead. "Why are you not listening to me doctor? You are killing me and my children."

Kenny let out another horrific scream and looked over at his mother in sheer terror and grief. He choked and gasped. He suddenly got very limp and still. He turned his head towards Jenny and looked straight into her eyes. He managed to force a weak smile at her. His voice became broken and frail.

He stretched out his weak hands toward her. "Mama! Mama! I love you, Mama... even though you did this to me. I still love you with all my heart. You will always be my Mama! Always!" Kenny closed his eyes and became completely still. He was gone.

Jenny's tears streamed as she sobbed with intense grief at seeing her baby boy die before her very eyes.

"I'm so sorry Kenny! So sorry Kaley! How was I to know this would happen to you? I love you both so very much." She laid there sobbing in unbelief and utter shock. The nurse and doctor went over to Kenny's stretcher with a giant medical instrument.

"Mrs Daniels, you might want to turn your head and not watch this part."

Jenny looked away briefly.

Snap! Snap! Snap!

The doctor had a giant sopher clamp with sharp teeth in his hand. Jenny couldn't see anything because the doctor and nurse were in the way. The computer monitor was showing in real-time a video graphic of a baby being dismembered in a womb and body parts being placed on a surgical plate where it was being reassembled and counted.

"Nurse, are all the body parts accounted for?"

The nurse finished counting, whispering the name of body parts as she took inventory. She looked up and smiled at the doctor. "Yes doctor, all parts are here! Can I prepare the fetal material for preserving for medical research and harvesting?"

The doctor looked at the surgical plate. "Yes, these are high quality intact specimens and should yield a fat bonus for both of us!"

The doctor grinned and gave a thumbs up gesture. "Very well done, Nurse! Another successful termination procedure!"

The doctor looked toward Jenny and then back at the nurse.

"The patient seemed a little more apprehensive and hostile than expected but I think it was just the jitters of going through with it. She will come around and thank us for removing this burden. I know she will."

Jenny laid there broken and conquered. She looked like a dead person, unable to move or respond as all her energies were zapped from the horror. She stared expressionless up at the grey ceiling, only residual tears intermittently ran down her cheeks.

The nurse rolled away the computer monitor cart to reveal Kenny's empty stretcher. The doctor finally came back over to Jenny with his clipboard in his hand. He smiled with plastic cordiality and professionalism. He spoke in the "I'm-Not-Just-A-Doctor-I'm-A-God" tone of voice.

"See now Mrs. Daniels. We know what's best for you! It wasn't that bad. The procedures were highly successful and without any real complications. You'll be free to go very soon. Oh, Mrs. Daniels, we do have counselors that will be happy to meet with you to discuss any mental stresses or psychological misgivings you might now have. How's that sound, my friend?"

Jenny looked at the doctor, her face changed from expressionless to sadness to then gritting teeth madness. She screamed so loud it reverberated throughout the clinic.

"Who gave you the right to take my children from me, doctor? Who gave you the right to kill my precious babies?"

The doctor rolled his eyes in a haughty gesture. He smiled, wagged his head and started thumbing through the sheets of paper on his clipboard.

"Well, Mrs Daniels to answer your question. Honestly, it was YOU that gave us the right to take your children from you. You told us that they were an inconvenience at this stage in your life. You told us it was YOUR body and YOUR reproductive rights! You said these babies would be a burden to your life ambitions, your financial goals and to your already hectic schedule. You said you didn't have time to be a mother right now. We didn't kill your babies. You did!"

Jenny laid there dazed and disbelieving at his words, shaking her head violently no. The doctor then shoved the clipboard up to Jenny's face.

"See this document right here Jenny? It has your signature on it! See the check-boxes above it? See the one marked LIFE and the one marked DEATH. You chose this one Jenny!"

The doctor pointed to the check-box marked DEATH with a check on it. "It was your right to choose, Jenny. Your right to choose and YOU CHOSE DEATH! You chose death... you chose DEATH Jenny!"

The Nightmare Reality

"YOU CHOSE DEATH!" Jenny awakened, startled by the words still echoing in her inner ear as she suddenly sat up in her bed.

"What a crazy nightmare!" She blurted under her breath. Shaking her head, Jenny began to call out for Travis. "Travis!"

She looked over to see that Travis was not there lying on his side of the bed. She then noticed that her whole bedroom furniture was different and things were completely arranged in an unfamiliar way. In her nightgown, Jenny slipped into a warmer, full bathrobe. She was clearly disturbed by all the changes that she noticed in her bedroom.

She then yelled out towards the master bathroom. "Travis, are you in the bathroom? What is going on here? Did you change all this in the middle of the night? How could you change our bedroo..." Jenny suddenly stopped in mid sentence as she looked around in utter disbelief at what she saw. She called out even louder for Travis. "Travis! Where are you?"

Jenny looked in her master bathroom to notice a totally elegant, remodeled space. She started to pinch herself and slap her face as she thought out loud. "I must still be dreaming. This can't be real. We could never afford this." Jenny peered out her bedroom window. She didn't see Mr. and Mrs. Apple Tree on the hillside where Travis and she planted them before the twins were born. "Over six year old trees-gone?" She puzzled. Jenny began to panic and her voice grew loud and shaky. "What! No way! What is going on here?"

Jenny rushed through the house calling for Travis and also for the twins. She opened every room which was much different from yesterday. Kenny's race car bedroom was now a guest bedroom that looked like a showroom with nice new furniture. Kaley's bedroom was no longer pink and girly with her pony collection but instead was a home office with desks, bookcases and computers in it.

She frantically called out for her family.

"Travis! Kaley! Kenny! Where are you all? Is this some weird and sick joke? So help me, when I find you all... How is this even possible?" Jenny looked in amazement at all her nice new stainless steel appliances and upgraded kitchen with beautiful stone quartz countertops. She called out in the emptiness of a gorgeous, elegant home.

"Travis, kids, I'm starting to get really freaked out now! I need you to come out, wherever you are! Please guys, Mama's not joking, I'm getting very scared." Jenny looked even more panicked as she opened the door to her front porch to see a completely outside remodeled home with a new roof, siding and window treatments.

The shrubbery and flowerbeds that she, the twins and Travis planted were no longer where they were yesterday. Jenny looked over to the driveway. She didn't see their older blue minivan but instead, in its place was a sparkling new candy apple Ferrari.

Jenny was visibly shaken to the core, her heart racing and becoming faint. She sat down on a chair on her front porch. She visibly slapped her face several times to try to wake herself up. "Wake up! Wake up Jenny!"

She whispered out loud her thoughts and prayers. "No way! I must still be dreaming. I need to wake up here. What is going on? I don't understand, God. This doesn't make any sense! Where's my family Where's my rickety ol' home? Where's my husband and the twins?"

Jenny continued to shake her head no as she entered back into the immaculate farmhouse. In the living room, the fireplace was now covered in beautiful rock work and the mantle was lovely laminated, carved wood with exposed grain. There was no picture of the twins above the fireplace. The Christmas tree was even very different. It was a little plastic one that had fixed LED lights and ornaments. There were no gifts under the tree except a single small gift, from herself to herself. She touched the gift without unwrapping it. Jenny frantically scurried through the house looking for anything that could be connected to Travis and the twins. She saw her phone and grabbed it. She looked for Travis's number but there was no contact information for him on her phone. She randomly called one of her old best friends from college- Lisa Kent. The phone rang and a female voice answered. "Hello. Hello, can I help you?"

Jenny blurted out. "Yes, Lisa it's me Jenny. I seem to be in the twilight zone here and freaking out right now. My family has totally vanished and my whole house is so different. I think I'm going crazy here." Lisa was taken back with a bit of confusion. "Jenny Abernathy is that you? Jenny, what are you talking about?"

"No Lisa, it's Jenny Daniels now. Abernathy was my maiden name."

"But I thought you went back to your maiden name?"

"Now Lisa, why on earth would I do that? You know better girl. What's going on here? I'm so scared! My family is nowhere to be found and my home is not the same!"

"Jenny, you must be relapsing again. You really need to call your doctor. I can't help you anymore."

"Relapsing? What are you talking about Lisa?"

"Jenny, I know you've had a lot of psychological challenges and I am sorry about your mixed up life now... I really am. But every time I've gotten involved, I end up making things worse. So please, just call your doctor. I gotta go now. Bye Jenny." Jenny heard a click on the other end of the line. She was even more scared and worried now. She frantically searched her phone again. She found her mother's number and called her.

"Hello, Jenny, what's up?"

Jenny breathed a sigh of relief at hearing her mother's voice.

"Mother! What's going on? Do you have the twins? Is Travis over there? Am I being pranked with some elaborate prank?"

"What are you talking about Jenny?"

"Am I going bonkers, Mother? I woke up this morning from a nightmare, mind you, and Travis and the twins are completely vanished and Grannygrans house looks like we hit the mega jackpot lottery! No broken down minivan... instead a beautiful Ferrari in the front driveway!"

The phone went silent. Jenny heard her mother whispering something to someone in the background. "Mother, who are you talking to and what s going on? Where is Travis and the kids?"

"Yes, Jenny my love, I heard you. I was just talking to Rick. Is there anyone with you?"

"No Mother, that's the friggin problem! Travis, Kaley and Kenny are nowhere to be found. It's like they don't even exist. It's insane!"

"Jenny, have you been taking your medication as prescribed by Dr. Shultz?

Jenny became irate and irritated. "Mother, I have never been on any kind of medication! What are you implying? That I really am crazy? Well, I'm not crazy Mom!"

Jenny started to break down in great sobs. Jenny's mother consoled her.

"Jenny, it's okay. Listen, please, can you drive here to Bloomington? I can help you and we can talk all about it when you get here, okay? Are you okay Jenny?"

"No, I'm not okay Mom! Everything is Helter Skelter. Kenny and Kaley, my babies are gone! Travis is gone! Apparently, I have plenty of money now... which doesn't feel right at all! Mr. and Mrs. Apple tree are also gone too. How could they just cut down those trees like that? They have so much sentimental value!"

"Please honey, come over here right now and we'll talk about it." Her Mom spoke firmly.

Jenny looked pathetically drained and confused. "Okay, I guess. Nothing makes sense to me anymore. I'm still dreaming a nightmare here! I'll be over as soon as I can! Bye!" Jenny pushed the end call button on her phone.

She scrambled around her bedroom to put on regular clothes. She was amazed at her vast wardrobe. She continued to marvel at all the fancy stuff she apparently has in her new and improved farmhouse.

She found the car keys to the Ferrari and spun out of her driveway. Speeding beyond the speed limit, Jenny drove ferociously towards her mother's home. She steamed with confusion and frustration, determined to find out what was happening to her. Jenny noticed everything on her way to her mother's seemed a bit off as well, peculiar differences from what she remembered just yesterday.

She finally made it to her mother's home, screeching her tires as she zipped into the driveway. She jumped out and went to the front door of the house. Her mother was waiting at the door. Jenny hugged her and spoke directly into her mother's concerned eyes. "Mother, please talk to me. What is going on? Everything is so different, like I've switch realities or fallen into a parallel universe where I have lots of money but no family! All my children's books I've been writing with Travis are gone. Instead, I have pictures on my walls with famous politicians and celebrities that I know I've never met! Plaques and awards on my wall congratulating me for championing women's rights issues... and even infanticide!"

Jenny's mother held her daughter's hand and shuttered visibly from her words. "Honey, you are not a children's book writer. Your downtown office secretaries do all your writing for you and..."

Jenny interrupted her. "What? No, Mom. I've started writing children's books with Travis and have a whole collection soon to be published. You know this! I've shown you them!"

Jenny's mother spoke soft but firmly, still holding Jenny's hand. "No, my love, you are the founder and director of your own nonprofit organization, The Woman's Advocacy & Rights Group, or WAR Group as you like to call it."

"What? No way Mother! I am not pro-choice, I'm pro-life! I gave up that way of thinking in college when I got serious with Travis and then pregnant, remember?"

"No Jenny, you are definitely not on your meds. You and Travis divorced over six years ago. Jenny, you are having another really bad episode."

"Divorced? Come on, Mom! Travis and I love each other so much. We've been together for over nine years and six of those year have been with our beautiful twins, Kaley and Kenny! You know this!"

Jenny began to tremble very forcefully and suddenly. She fell into a heap on the floor.

Jenny's mother began to gently caress her hair. She looked genuinely worried as she tried to get her daughter to come to grips with reality.

"Jenny, I'm sorry but we must confront this head on- you gave up the twins, remember darling? You had both of the abortions here in Bloomington at the university clinic.

Jenny suddenly burst out in a fit of passion. "Abortions? No, no, no Mom! I had those babies and have raised them with Travis in Grannygran's old farmhouse. They just turned six last May and they are beautiful children! No, Mom, don't try to tell me this. It's a lie! You can't tell me all these memories I have of them are a lie, Mother!"

Jenny covered her face and then tearfully looked at her mother. "Mother, you think I'm crazy, don't you? Am I crazy, Mother? Am I?"

Jenny's mother hugged her frazzled daughter. "No, my love you're not crazy... you're just very confused and dealing with these unresolved issues, that's all. You still have a lot of guilt with some self made fantasies that always seem to surface during the holidays... which is close to the anniversary of the first..." She suddenly stopped speaking and looked away and down.

Jenny looked at her mother, expecting her to finish her sentence. "The anniversary of the first what, Mother? The first abortion! I didn't have any abortions! I did not kill my babies!"

Jenny's mother raised up a little, getting a bit unnerved and defensive at her daughter's remarks. "Jenny, don't talk like that! You didn't kill them. You terminated your pregnancies. You had every right to do that and you know this! You are a Pro Choice champion and voice for all women. Your whole career is based on this. You need to really get a grip and fast... because you don't need any negative publicity since your whole life and livelihood is based on woman's issues and their abortion rights!"

Jenny shook her head vigorously. "Mother! This is not only sad for me but for you too! I remember very well helping you come to see abortion as wrong after the twins were born... now you've reverted back and are trying to tell me that I killed my children and am a militant advocate for abortion rights! I feel very sick and this can't be my reality. It just can't be!" Jenny broke down in tears again.

"Those were very traumatic times back then for you Jenny. I know you've had deep regrets but this is the first time you have gone so overboard with your alternate reality, fantasy episodes. If you don't get a handle on this soon, you're gonna have to be hospitalized Jenny... and I don't want that for you or think this would be good for your career, your reputation and image, especially with all the grants and donations you receive."

"My career, Mother? My reputation? You are telling me that my beautiful twins are dead and I should be worried about my career, Mother!"

Jenny's mother shuddered, visibly shaken. She offered her daughter some pills to take. "Jenny, my love, you are having a serious bad episode. I need you to take these. They will help you relax, put you in a right frame of mind and you will feel better."

Jenny pushed her Mom's hand away. "I don't want medication to make me feel better, Mother! I want my children back! I want Travis. How can I feel better knowing I took the life of my lovely son and daughter?"

"You must learn to accept your decision as the right choice for you then and now. You can't take it back, Jenny."

Jenny started to choke up. "I want my family back! I want my Travis back. I need my Kenny, my Kaley, my beautiful twins. Mother, they're so beautiful. If you could see them... as I know them. You love them too. They know you as Grammy. If you could only see them, what they've become, you would..." Jenny's words crashed into heavy sobs.

Her mother's own hardened look broke as she embraced her daughter with sympathy.

"I know you... must have loved them in some way... and I am sure I would have loved them as my grandchildren too... but no regrets Jenny." Both of them stayed embraced for a long moment. Jenny finally wiped her cheeks and looked straight into her mother's eyes. "Where's Travis now Mother? I need to see Travis."

"No, Jenny that's a very bad idea. You can't go see him."

"Mother, I need to see him. If I can just talk with Travis... I know

I could... Maybe I could... maybe I could find real closure! Maybe I could finally let it go for once and for all, Mother. Please, tell me where he is and I promise I will not bring any of this up anymore. I will somehow... let it go."

Jenny's mother was very hesitant. "I don't know Jenny. I don't know how it would help you... and I don't think you will like what you find."

"What? Mother, please..."

"Travis is remarried and lives near Highland Village."

"Remarried? How do you know this?" Jenny asked.

"I bumped into him with his family in the grocery store about a year ago."

Jenny visibly deflated. "It can't be, Mother. I was with him just yesterday with the twins having a snowball fight. We..."

Jenny's mother interrupted. "Jenny, honey... You divorced him just months after the last abortion. He remarried two years after that. It's been many years now. He's actually a young pastor of a small church on the other side of town."

"Mother, do you have an address?"

Jenny's mother shook her head no. "Jenny, let it be my love. Let it be."

"No Mom, please... if what you say is true and you want me to have real closure, I must see him for myself."

Jenny's mother surrendered. "I think his phone and address maybe in the phone directory."

Jenny scampered to a drawer and found the directory and thumbed through it. She found Travis's contact information and scribbled it down on a napkin.

Her mother stood shaking her head in disapproval. Jenny turned and kissed her mother. Her mother chided her like she would a small child. "Jenny, don't make a scene with him. Just get the closure you need and come back here right away. A northern cold front is suppose to come in later tonight so you don't want to get caught out in it. Come back here, you can spend the night here with us if you want."

Jenny affirmed her words. "It will be okay Mom. I promise... I will get to the bottom of all this and I will let it all go. Maybe I will come back tonight or for sure tomorrow, okay?" Her mother nodded as Jenny rushed out the door. She fired up her Ferrari and took off like a bat out of Hell. She drove through the city of Bloomington like she was on autopilot mode.

Jenny began having flashbacks of all her memories with Travis and the twins. A flashback of when the twins were born and Travis's excitement showing off digital photos of them to every stranger in the hospital and then posting them on every social media platform available. A flashback of when Kenny and Kaley were less than six months old. Both of them were side by side in their crib with their little arms naturally hugging each other... and Travis and Jenny quickly snapping that Kodak moment before they woke up. A flashback of the day Kaley took her first steps and how Kenny took his first steps soon after with the help of his sister. A flashback of the twin's third birthday and how she dressed them up as cute sunflowers. A flashback of the first day of Kindergarten when Kenny had to sit next to his sister so he wouldn't be scared anymore.

As Jenny drove methodically, she recalled these memories with both joy and sorrow, bursts of laugher fizzling into tears. Her car's on-board GPS finally snapped her back into reality- It robotically spoke "You have arrived at your destination."

Jenny looked at the mailbox number and the modest home that sat on a cul de sac. She noticed a little child's swing set out in the front yard. She sat in her Ferrari with her arms draped around the steering wheel for a few minutes just musing, staring at the house. Jenny shook her head in a gesture of self doubt. She heard herself ask, "What are you doing here Jenny?"

Questionable Answers

Jenny impulsively jumped out of her Ferrari. She zipped up her winter coat as it started to get more chilly outside. She walked briskly toward the house but slowed down as she got closer. On the door she noticed a beautiful Christmas wreath. Jenny started to reach to ring the doorbell but then suddenly turned completely back around to leave.

Pushing away her inhibitions, she turned again to the door and quickly hit the buzzer. Susan Daniels answered the door with a baby all bundled up in her arms and a toddler boy was close by, clinging onto her leg. Susan looked at Jenny with an air of familiarity, as if she knew who Jenny was. Intrigued, she spoke between the screen door.

"Oh hello, what can we do for you?"

Jenny struggled to find the words. "I was um... I was wondering if Travis Daniels lives here?"

Travis walked up to the door just as Jenny finished asking. "Who is it honey?" Travis saw Jenny and visibly sputtered. His eyes widened and then he went completely silent. Jenny changed quick glances at him. She looked complexed and bewildered. He looked shocked to see her.

"Travis, can I talk to you for a moment? We can talk outside here. I just need to ask you a couple questions then be on my way."

Travis exchanged glances at Susan who had moved out of the doorway. Susan nodded her head and gave a look of approval at Travis. "Wow, Jenny... It's been... a long time since I've seen you. But yea, sure. Let me get a jacket though." Susan handed Travis a jacket which he quickly put on. His toddler son was clinging to him.

"Kenny, you need to stay inside with Mama. Daddy will be right back, okay?"

Little Kenny nodded and walked away. "Okay Daddy."

Jenny gave him a token smile. She then turned to Travis. "Did you say... Kenny?"

Travis pushed Kenny towards his mother and slowly shut the door behind him. "Oh, yes, that right. That's my son Kenny. We named him after my grandfather."

"Yes, I knew that... I mean, I knew your grandfather was named Kenneth."

Travis looked intently in Jenny's eyes trying to discern her visit. He saw her broken countenance and discerned her sadness. He was pleasant and nominally smiled back. There was an awkward silent moment between them.

"Soooo... Jenny, it seems like forever and a day since I saw you last. I saw your mother sometime ago at Shopmart. How... How are you doing these days?"

Jenny strained to keep her composure and her tears at bay as she resisted the urge to throw herself completely in his arms. She recognized that he was not the same Travis that she knew just yesterday.

"Travis, I, I don't know who I am anymore. I seem to have lost my way and... lost my mind. I don't know. Just yesterday I had a beautiful family. But today I'm all alone with just a past that haunts me. My whole life seems to have changed in one moment in time... in a choice or choices that I made. I came over here to see you in hopes that my nightmare would somehow go away but instead it's like... it's even worse."

Travis's face saddened and looked genuinely concerned. "Oh I am so sorry to hear that Jenny... I didn't know you had a family. What happened to them?"

Jenny shook her head no. "No, I guess I'm confusing this situation even more. Apparently, I guess I never really ever had a family. I guess I've been living in some sort of fantasy world or something. You see, I have these very vivid memories that people are telling me were never real."

Jenny stared blankly towards Travis but offset slightly as she gathered her thoughts.

"Like what kind of memories, Jenny?" Travis was intrigued.

"Memories of you... and me... and the twins, Kenny and Kaley. We live in my grandmother's old farmhouse. We are a family, I mean, we were a family."

Travis blinked his eyes and shook his head in unbelief and sadness at what he heard Jenny say.

"Oh my goodness, Jenny. I am so sorry you are having some real issues from the abortion trauma you went through. I never realized you had named our unborn children, Jenny. Even after we got divorced, I thought you still referred to them as 'its' rather than human beings... you know, according to your pro-choice perspective."

Jenny looked intently at Travis and began to speak passionately. "But don't you remember Travis, I let go of that ideology. You helped me see the light. I became pro-life because of you!"

Travis's eyes widened. "I wish it were true, Jenny. I really do. We married on an impulse and we were so very young. We were in love but we hardly knew each other's background. Don't you remember us fighting all the time? You were so headstrong. You could never see my conservative perspective on the issues."

Travis looked away from Jenny, towards the ground and shuffled his feet and then continued. "Jenny, you seem to have completely put that period of your life out of your memory... and maybe that's for the better, really."

"No Travis, I need to remember what really happened to us. I need to be made to remember! I can't live in fantasy land anymore! I can't believe in a lie anymore, if this is what it is..."

Travis looked at her more compassionately, discerning her pain and mental anguish. "You really don't remember, Jenny? How can you have completely forgotten? He looked for any spark of memory in her eyes and saw none. "You know that first abortion was so sad and crazy.

It was during Christmas break. Actually, five days before Christmas to be exact. Come to think of it, it was seven years ago today exactly... December 20th... That's why you've shown up today, isn't it, Jenny?"

"I don't know Travis. I am trying to make sense of things but it seems to be more confusing as I go along here. The more answers I get, the more questions I have!" Jenny looked to the ground.

Travis sighed. "You know Jenny, it ruined our Christmas that year... and mine for many years to come. First, we thought you were carrying only one child at the time. We both had been pretty stressed about it... with college and our carefully laid out plans. A child was not in the mix of things. Not for you, or me really. But I was on the fence, yet more against abortion than for it. I tried to convince you to at least go full term and give the baby up for adoption. We fought about it many times. That's why you didn't do it sooner. I think you were around your 16th week of pregnancy when you insisted that a child would ruin your future goals as a social worker, as a political activist and your work with that very militant pro-choice group you had become apart of on campus. I thought you wanted to be the poster child besides the brain child for that group!"

Travis scanned Jenny's face for some sort of eye contact that showed her remembering but there was nothing there. "You don't remember anything?"

" I'm sorry. I don't."

"Anyways, after so much fighting, I finally gave in to you. I went against my own conscience. I went along with the abortion because I loved you and wanted to make you happy. But the abortion procedure was not without incident, Jenny. Somehow you had a bad reaction to the medicine they gave you before the procedure began. You were unconscious for a good while in the clinic as they tried to wake you up. When you finally came to, they rushed the procedure since they had other abortions scheduled to perform. Apparently, to make sure they got the clinic's daily quota in. In the rush, somehow they failed to realize that you had another baby inside of you. Yes, you were carrying twins, Jenny. I guess this is why you now entertain ideas of us as a family with twins."

Travis stopped suddenly.

41

"Please, Travis, go on. Please tell me. I need to really know... to remember."

"Anyways, the doctor had given you post abortion medication. He stated that one of the side effects to it was that you might gain a little weight. So we didn't think too much of it when you still gained weight and seemed to get bigger. It was almost three months later that we were shocked to discover another baby was kicking inside your belly!"

Jenny shook her head as if she was in total denial but listened on.

"I know it sounds crazy Jenny but you know it's happened before with other women who had mistakenly only aborted one of their twins too. At first, we thought it was perhaps a new pregnancy altogether even though we were using contraceptives. But your doctor confirmed it was from the first pregnancy. Now you were around seven months pregnant, with a baby boy, Jenny!"

Travis again hesitated. "Jenny, it was this second child, the abortion of this baby that drove the nail into the coffin of our marriage. You were so fixated on terminating this second child who had survived the first abortion. I had regretted the first abortion so much. I thought the discovery of a second child, our son, was God's way of giving us a second chance and healing our fractured marriage. But you were set on terminating him as well. This ripped our already fragile relationship totally apart. And when you lied to me and went to the clinic without my approval and got a partial birth abortion procedure done, I was furious and left you. Jenny, you may not remember, but I do... you became a very hard and bitter person then. The last thing I ever told you, I yelled from the phone. I told you that the first abortion was perhaps manslaughter by ignorance but the second, made it a cold blooded double homicide! I also yelled at you that a man's right to choose should also be considered along with a woman's since it's both our offspring. I moved out of your grandmother's house. You were the one who actually filed for a divorce six weeks later... and we have never spoken another word until today, Jenny."

Travis spoke softly. "I think it's the best thing for you Jenny, to forget about our lives back then and this made up fantasy about our children being born to us... and to move on with your life."

Jenny started to intermittently cry between the words she

uttered. "No Travis, I want to remember but not this... I want to remember my life with my twins and with you! I don't know any other life here and now. But apparently, I'm a total delusional nut job, crazy person and still in a hyper-state of denial about what could have been... what should have been... our little family, our lives together with those babies!"

Travis shook his head briskly. "I don't know how to respond to that Jenny. It has taken years for me to know God's forgiveness, to forgive myself and to even forgive you Jenny. I once despised you for everything during that time... how you even profited from the whole ordeal by winning that large sum of money from the lawsuit against the clinic. But I now ask you to forgive me as I have forgiven you about these things. I know that it was also my decision, Jenny... the first abortion, I mean. I went along with the abortion. It was a huge mistake and in my judgment, the greatest sin I ever committed against God. God has let me see my sin. Shame and guilt I know are considered psychological enemies to this post modern culture where nothing is taboo or wrong... but they are really very healthy emotions for the conscience, otherwise we keep making wrong choices. But I now know forgiveness. God has given me grace to let it go."

Travis stared directly in Jenny's eyes. "We cannot change the past Jenny. We can only change ourselves now. We can only make right choices in the present."

Jenny nodded. "But why can't I have a second chance? Can't there be a way we can go back and do it differently?" She abruptly answers herself. "Don't worry about answering that. I'm just venting here..."

Travis spoke his words carefully. "Second chances are so rare in this world. Many choices, many actions are permanent things that can never be undone. We normally don't get second chances, Jenny... only a second opportunity to make a better decision concerning a similar matter. But first choices are as abundant as the sand on the shore. When a choice must be made, we must make it so that there are no regrets or wishing for second chances."

Jenny knew he was right but still couldn't believe her reality. "I wish I could make the choice again. I wish I could choose... I would choose life. I would choose to keep our babies!"

Travis let out a sigh of relief. "Jenny, I am so glad you see that now. You know, it really isn't about a woman's right to choose but about a woman's choice to do what is right! The supreme court of the United States has no authority to legalize what is already self evident as a crime against humanity. There is a higher court that must be considered. There really is no argument on a woman's free will to choose to abort her baby as there is no argument against a man's free will to go on a killing rampage at a shopping mall. But free will does not make it right. Just because a corrupt justice system legalizes immorality that shouldn't entitle or enable us to do what we know deep down is wrong."

Jenny sniffled. "I know I was once so mixed up about all these things... about when a life begins and when a fetus becomes a viable baby with human rights... but I thought you convinced me Travis so many years ago."

"Jenny, I wish I had. Do you not remember when I told you that even a child knows the answer to when life begins? A child knows that a seed planted in fertile ground when it starts to grow within the soil can plainly deduct that life has begun for that seedling. But even our highest court in the land can't make that simple deduction about a human embryo? It is utter madness and willful denial of basic truth. All of science, biology, medical knowledge, philosophy and even the laws of physics cry out in defense of the unborn. Without a shadow of a doubt, human life begins at the very onset of conception. Yet we have a good part of our society that radically and militantly denies these obvious facts... and why Jenny, because we have become a self centered, indulgent society that would rather violently sacrifice the life of a child than take responsibility for our immoral actions." Travis continued.

"I argued these points with you Jenny and yet you wouldn't listen to me then. You were so set in your ways. I went along with the first abortion and had no power to stop the second. You know Jenny, I lived with our children's ghosts haunting my conscience too for a very long time but forgiveness is real. I am glad you are coming to terms with your past actions and perspectives but you must learn forgiveness from God and with yourself now... and move on with your life. It's the only way not to go crazy."

Jenny looked deep into Travis's eyes. "I know this now, Travis. I heard your arguments back in college and I thought I really changed for you and for God." Jenny paused and Travis continued.

"Jenny, I can hardly bring myself to remember or to speak of our children either, really. I must accept forgiveness and move on. It's the only way I can now function as a human being or I would still to this day be wallowing in my own guilt and shame."

"Travis, I can't let it go though. I don't want to let it go. I like the family I have... in my, in my dreams, I guess. But I can't go back, can I?"

"Pray to God, I wish we could, Jenny. But the past will always eat you up if you do not give it to God. Once I was able to do that, God healed me and now I have a family. I am a father... something I had always longed to be... even when I was with you, Jenny. But you need to let God erase your past and then He will draw you a new future. Please, let it go and let God, my friend."

Jenny struggled to get her words out. "I guess... I can try... but I need to go now. Thank you again, Travis... and may God bless you and your family." Jenny swiftly ended the conversation as she turned away towards her Ferrari. Travis looked on with sympathy at Jenny leaving so broken and alone. He called out to her. "Please be careful Jenny, go with God, my friend. I will pray for you... and please try... to have... a merry Christmas."

Travis knew his holiday benediction crashed and burned to the ground. Jenny spun back around, with tears running down her face. "I don't think I can ever have a merry Christmas, Travis. I am damned to spend the holidays in a state of perpetual guilt and mourning over the choices I made. I will forever have my babies in my memory during every Christmas season!"

Travis looked down at the frosty ground. Then he looked back up, straight into Jenny's sad eyes and with compassion said, "I don't believe that Jenny. I believe that forgiveness is more powerful than our bad choices. The only thing more powerful than forgiveness is the power to make the right choice the first time and never need forgiveness to begin with. But since you can not go back, you must go forward, Jenny. You too can be forgiven! You too can learn to forgive yourself!" Travis's words were like a crackling fire on a cold winter's night.

"I believe that you can truly have a merry Christmas, Jenny. If you focus not on your past choice or even on our babies who never were born to this world... but on the true meaning of Christmas... on the one baby that was born to this world... Jesus, so that we all could know the wonderful, liberating power of forgiveness from our wrong choices!"

Jenny visibly relaxed and seemed more surrendered from her turmoil as she responded serene and softly. "Thank you Travis. I appreciate your words. I always have, deep down... really."

Jenny gave Travis a longing look. She wanted to hug him like she had always remembered but knew it must not be appropriate. Travis discerned her extreme loneliness. He reached over and gave her a consoling hug.

He then whispered in her ear. "Our children are okay, Jenny. They are in the very bosom of God now, in the full trust of the Father's care and they are waiting for us... to fully place our heart's there too... in the Father's care. Someday, Jenny, you and I, we will see our children once again! You wait and see!"

Travis smiled and winked with a tear in his eye. "Jenny, the measure of God's mercy goes far beyond the measure of our sins, remember that!"

Jenny needed those words. She nodded humbly with no more words or fight of her own. She turned and walked back to her Ferrari. Travis watched her drive away in the cold of snow before heading back into his house.

Jenny drove many miles to nowhere as the weather turned more ominous. She kept thinking about her real life now... or the lack thereof. She could not understand how she had so many vivid memories of something so unreal, so made up in her head. She still felt like she was in a nightmare, with no way of ever waking up.

Full Empty Life

After a long and dreary ride, Jenny found herself back at her modernized farmhouse outside of Ellettsville. She went inside the lavished home and a sense of deep loneliness gripped her soul as she took inventory of her situation. It was as if she had just experienced the loss of her whole family for the first time. She mulled about her beautiful, captivating house with no delight in its sparkle or bling bling.

Jenny saw that she was a very successful person in this reality. She had everything she had ever yearned for... but without her beautiful family, it was the most empty poverty she had ever known. Money, things, prestige, it was all a lie. Jenny contemplated that when you lay your head down on a pillow at night from whatever dream one is chasing, it is no dream without someone to share it with.

She also realized that all the liberal views about a woman's right to choose were nothing but a sham and a shame. No one has the right to choose death for another person, especially one's own unborn, defenseless child. "How could I have fallen for such ideas and perspectives?" She thought.

It was now night again. Jenny peered out the window to see a new snow falling. The arctic storm was now arriving. Jenny closed her eyes and saw Kaley and Kenny smiling and waving at her in their coats, mittens and their winter hats to keep warm. She saw Travis, Frostypants the snowman and the snowball fight. She chuckled out loud at the memory of fun and laughter they had. "But it wasn't real, Jenny!" Her thoughts damned her.

Sniffles of tears again broke the silence of the house. Jenny couldn't live like this for too long. She knew what she would have to do. But for now she would just cry. She found herself in the living room sprawled on the carpet weeping until she could weep no more.

Jenny finally pushed herself to get up and walked around her lonely home again. She went into Kaley's room filled with everything imaginable. She found endless books and materials on pro-choice and abortion clinic materials. She found letters from champion advocates and political leaders of pro-choice addressing her as a great asset to the cause of a woman's right to choose. Empty praises and accolades from empty people. After reading the letters and some of the material, Jenny realized that those who purport such ideas had to be miserable and lonely creatures like herself. How can anyone believe this stuff without a true disconnect to family values and honorable, decent things? Why had she bought into the lie, hook line and sinker, that children were inconvenient things and burdens?

All Jenny could remember about her children were that they brought her unending joy and blessing. She couldn't believe that she had really dove head first into liberal, pro-choice thinking. She could have sworn that Travis's conservative Christian upbringing had influenced her and brought her to understand the truth about abortion.

Jenny rummaging through her stuff, found a t-shirt that read "I had an abortion and it was fabulous!" in the front and "Not Ashamed!" on the back of it. She immediately felt faint, turned red and began to vomit profusely after reading it. She used the t-shirt to then clean up her vomit. She threw it in her trash compactor.

Jenny walked into what was once Kenny's room. As soon as she did, the emotions overwhelmed her as she remembered Kenny's little race car bed. She remembered the collection of matchbox cars that lined the walls on the tiny shelves that Travis had made for him.

Jenny went to his window and peered out into the backyard remembering the spot where the twins had played so much. She was amazed that she contained so many tears, so many memories... apparently not real. Her vision became blurred from the seeping tears of sadness until she looked down on the window sill. There she saw something that caught her eye like a firebrand. At first glance, she dismissed it as a pebble or some sort of debris. But as she studied it through her tears, she noticed it looked like a seed but not just any seed, an apple seed... Kenny's apple seed?

Curiosity overcame her and she reached for it. Jenny examined it closely and it was indeed an apple seed, a slightly sprouting apple seed! She remembered that Kenny had lost his apple seed in his room and was searching for it last night... in her false memories, in her "alternate reality". But what did this really mean now? If her memories of Kaley and Kenny were all made up, then how did this apple seed get here?

Jenny was confused. She didn't want to try to figure it out anymore. It would be just another deluded rabbit trail of questions that she would go down leading to emptiness and heartache.

The apple seed was surely a rip in the fabric of her reality. She strained her brain a little. "What was the last conversation between her and Kenny about the apple seed?" Jenny worked her mind to remember. The memory finally flashed before her. He was crying, searching for the apple seed in his room. "Kenny, what are you doing, my love?"

"I'm looking for my apple seed Mama. I didn't want to kill it. I don't want it to die."

"Oh honey! It's okay, my love. You didn't kill it! We'll look for your apple seed tomorrow and it won't die, I promise my love. We ll find your apple seed and give him a second chance! How bout that? Your apple seed will live!"

"You promise?"

"I promise!"

Jenny broke her flashback and took the seed and put it in her pocket. She went to the living room and the silence was deafening as she clung to a pillow on her couch. She began to be enraged that she had found the apple seed while crying. It was as if God was taunting her sorrow. Jenny became irate and started not thinking clearly at all. Her lonely madness drove a stake in her sorrow.

Jenny began trashing her beautiful home. "It's a lie... it's all a lie. I don't care for any of this stuff!" Jenny smashed beautiful Chinaware and broke furniture. She became so frantic and frenzied. She then searched the medicine cabinet in her bathroom to discover an old but full bottle of sedatives hiding behind some bathroom items.

"I guess if this is going to be my life then I deserve to die like my children!" Jenny raged out loud. "God, I can't accept your forgiveness or mine. I don't want to be forgiven! What I want is to never have killed my babies in the first place! Why didn't you stop me? Why didn't you put something in my way to show me the truth?" Jenny ranted on as she began to unhesitatingly gulp down a handful of the sedatives. "I don't want to live with the consequences! I deserve to die!"

Jenny anguished as she gulped down another handful with water. She had now taken the whole bottle.

She looked out the window to see the hill. She remembered where the snow angel family once laid from her false memories.

Jenny hastily put on her coat and gloves. She flung opened the door to her house with the cold and wind raging around her, inside of her.

She ran over to the hillside and plopped down on the snow bed. She began to flap her arms and legs to make a snow angel. She began to try to catch the snowflakes with her tongue in her blind madness.

In a moment she broke from her rage and began to mourn her existence. She looked up at the night sky, dark and foreboding. Shivering, Jenny prayed in a broken surrender. "Please God, forgive me for taking my life now. I don't deserve to live or even want to live with this guilt anymore."

The sedatives she took began to hit her hard. She was fading fast. "I am sorry God. I took my children's lives and now I'm taking mine. Please, just take away my sin and my shame."

Jenny slurred her words as she ended her prayer laying there on the snowy hill, inside the angel she had made. It was only a few moments later when Jenny began to really fade to black.

However, just before she did, she looked to the left of her to see Kaley smiling, laying next to her. She then looked to the right and there Kenny was smiling at her also. Jenny knew it was a delusion.

She wanted to speak, to move but she couldn't. The sedatives were overpowering her.

Jenny turned her head to Kaley who was smiling brightly as she grabbed and squeezed her mother's hand. "Mama, the only thing more powerful than forgiveness is the power to make the right choice the first time and never need forgiveness!" Kaley beamed.

Jenny sleepily shook her head "yes" to affirm Travis's words echoing through her Kaley.

Then Kenny squeezed her other hand. "Mama, remember you promised me that you would give my apple seed a second chance?" Kenny whispered and smiled.

Jenny was fading fast now. It was like a dream.

"Here's your second chance, Mama! Here's your second chance!" Both Kenny and Kaley softy spoke in unison as they squeezed Jenny's hands in the snow. Jenny barely heard those words when she slipped away... slipped away in the coldness, in the whiteout of the snow... to who knows where?

Second Chance First Choice

Sometimes the choices we make can come down hard on us, like a sudden winter storm.

A moment we can't take back, forever frozen in our hearts, never to thaw, never to warm.

Like ice makes sludge and regret makes pain, we tromp through life as if it is all we will ever know.

But then God sees through the frosted lens of our bleak humanity, sending mercy and hope, angels in the snow.

Jenny focused her eyes on the intense brightness of the lights. As things came into view she realized she was again in some sort of a hospital room. By the sound of the medical staff scurrying about, she knew that her suicide attempt must have failed. She opened her eyes more widely and tried to move her head a little. Then with a fright, a nurse came to her side. It was the same nurse from her previous nightmare. Jenny blinked her eyes to try to wake up.

The nurse called a doctor over to her side. Jenny could see from the corner of her eye the doctor coming towards her bed. It was the same doctor also from her nightmare!

Jenny jolted in horror like she had been struck by lightening.

"Doctor, the patient is waking up now. She seems to be having some sort of disturbing fit." The nurse shouted.

The doctor grabbed a hold of Jenny's shoulder to try to get her to calm down.

"What is going on here?" Jenny screamed as she sat up in her bed.

She was not strapped to the stretcher as in her previous nightmare.

"Honey, you've had a really bad reaction to the sedatives we gave you. You've been out like a brick for over an hour now."

"What sedatives? The sedatives from the bottle I took?" Jenny was confused.

The nurse looked at Jenny's complexed face.

"No, the ones we gave to you to help you relax and sedate you in preparation to perform the procedure."

"What procedure? No, no more nightmares!" Jenny screamed with such distraught.

The doctor looked flushed at Jenny's ignorance. "Mrs. Daniels, you are here for the vacuum aspiration procedure!"

"What?"

"The vacuum aspiration procedure to terminate your pregnancy. We need you to calm down so that we can start." The doctor spoke with dry professionalism.

"What? No way! You called me Mrs. Daniels?" Jenny's heart began to race.

"You mean...you haven't done it yet?" Jenny burst out.

The doctor looked down at the ground.

"No, I'm sorry. You had a severe reaction to the sedatives we gave you and you fell totally unconscious. We've been waiting for you to revive."

"You mean my babies are still inside of me?" Jenny clutched her abdomen which was a little extended. Her eyes went bright and wide. She looked over at a small mirror in the room. She was young, like when she was in college.

"I'm sorry Mrs. Daniels. It's this clinic's policy not to perform the procedure unless the patient is fully conscious and aware at all times. I am truly sorry but we can begin when you calm down now. We need to get back on schedule because we have many more patients and procedures to perform besides yours." The doctor was apologetic and hurried.

Jenny couldn't believe her ears. She sat up numb realizing her situation. She remembered it all now. She was still in college! She was at the clinic for the very first abortion!

"Mrs. Daniels, can we proceed with the injection? You will have to lay back down." The doctor instructed.

Jenny jumped off the bed quicker than a ray of light in her hospital gown.

"No thank you, doctor! I'm keeping my twins, my beautiful babies!" Jenny screamed loud enough for the whole clinic to hear.

Her heart soared above the clinic room now. All her deepest sorrow turned into the most joyous elation. It was all a sedated dream/ nightmare. Jenny looked all aglow now and tears of happiness began to cover her face as she lifted her head toward heaven. "Thank you God... oh thank you God! Thank you angels, thank you!"

The doctor and nurse both seemed surprised and much shaken by her sudden and unnerving outbursts. "Mrs. Daniels, you need to calm down and rethink this. You've had some sort of bad reaction or experience here. You are being irrational now." The doctor spoke firmly.

Jenny turned to the doctor with fire in her eyes. She took a deep breath. She knew now that she was fully alive and fully not dreaming!

"No doctor, you are irrational! How can you kill innocent babies every day in this very room and call it a procedure! You use your little nice medical terminologies to sanitize your barbaric bloody practices!" The doctor and nurse became even more shocked. The nurse began to fidget and become visibly disturbed.

"Mrs. Daniels, what has gotten into you? You are an up and rising crusader and a staunch advocate for the pro-choice movement. You've even done some PR for this clinic! What are you talking about? I've never seen you speak so, so..." The doctor was flushed with anger.

But Jenny was a fireball. "You know what's gotten into me, doctor? My twin babies have gotten into me! They spoke to me when

I was unconscious on that bed right there. I just lived a lifetime of memories with my children. They told me they wanted to give me a second chance! And that's now my first and only choice!" Jenny's tears flowed.

"I see now doctor, the evil of such an ideology that makes it lawful for a woman to kill her baby. You hide behind nice terminologies like "Planned Parenthood" when it is the exact opposite, more like planned infanticide and the making of childless mothers and fathers! How the demons must laugh at our pathetic language semantics. It's like calling a divorce lawyer, a marriage counselor! Or when we defend a woman's so called 'reproductive rights' but what we are actually defending is her un-reproductive 'wrongs' to kill her unborn child! Pregnant women are being used for political agendas and their babies led to the slaughter for profit. This is what I know is going on!"

The nurse began to visibly cry now. The doctor was immensely agitated as he motioned the nurse to get a grip on her composure.

"Obviously, you have had a very bad experience and some sort of sedative based delusional episode, Mrs. Daniels. You keep saying twin babies. You only have a single fetus according to the sonogram we did."

"You are wrong doctor. I see how your staff rush through those sonograms and ultrasound procedures. Check it again. You're staff is always in a hurry due to your business incentives of trying to meet quotas... of how many abortions you want to do each day. Life is not the option you promote here because it hurts your pocketbook. You mostly encourage death because it's your money maker. So please, forgive me for being blunt honest but I know the scam well since I have been a part of it! Anyways doctor, I know I have fraternal twins in me, a boy and a girl!" Jenny looked for the clothes she had on when she came into the clinic.

"Well, whatever you want to think but something has set you off your natural disposition. But I'm afraid you are going have to calm down and reevaluate your decision to come here. However, you are upsetting my staff so I am asking you to please leave the clinic immediately. Perhaps you can rethink your new revelation. We can discuss your condition and reschedule the procedure at a later time." The doctor then motioned the nurse to get Jenny's change of clothes.

"No doctor, don't you worry about 'my condition'. My condition is a blessing from God and I will never have to rethink or reschedule this again."

"Whatever, you say Mrs. Daniels. But your husband Travis is out in the lobby with his hands wringing with worry, thinking that you are having an abortion right now. We have tried to let him know that a delay has kept us from finishing the procedure but he is fully expecting you to terminate this pregnancy. He may be sorely disappointed."

The doctor began to head out of the room for Jenny to change and to also go over the last ultrasound video images of her pregnancy. Jenny's sudden emphatic assertion that she was with twins had rattled him a little. Jenny froze with pure excitement at hearing Travis's name. She spoke to the nurse who was now helping her.

"My husband... Oh Travis... I know he really was just going along with my decision. I know he will be okay, I know it." Jenny went inside a cubicle and hurriedly changed back into her clothes. She again held her extended abdomen and began to tear up again. She whispered to her belly in the solitude of the moment, "I am so sorry Kaley and Kenny. I almost lost you! Thank you for being my angels in the snow, watching over me. I love you both so much!"

Jenny looked up toward heaven again. "And thank you for this chance, whether it's my first or second... it's my chance and it's my choice and I thank you God!"

Jenny reached for the lobby door. She had gone so far, seen so much and changed so drastically in such a short time. A lifetime in a moment. She wiped her eyes dry and walked through the lobby decorated with Christmas lights and holiday decor.

Travis was sitting there, just as the doctor said, wringing his hands and worried. He was wearing a suit jacket with his tie untied and draped next to him on a chair. His face was unshaven with stubby, patchy areas. Jenny always made fun of his struggling musician appearance. Travis looked up to see Jenny approaching. He immediately sighed and was visibly relieved to see her. Jenny lit up to see Travis so young and handsome. She also noticed that he too brightened to see her. "So how did things go in there? I mean, I thought I heard you scream a few times. Is everything alright? Did the um,... procedure go okay?"

Travis handed Jenny her coat jacket.

Jenny didn't answer. She just threw her arms around him, kissed him and smelled his neck.

Tears welled up again in her eyes.

"Are you okay, Jenny?" Travis seemed to get the worried look back on his face.

"I'm very fine, my love. Please, let's get out of here. I have so much to tell you but not here... not here."

A moment later a nurse briskly walked up to Jenny and placed a note from the doctor in her hand. The note just read, "After a cross examination of your most recent ultrasound and images, I believe you are in fact carrying two fetuses after all. Please advise us of your intentions."

Jenny handed the note back to the nurse. "I already knew this and my intentions are never to step foot in this clinic again. Thank you!"

The nurse left in a hurry. Travis looked curiously at Jenny who was beaming with a strange joy and tranquility. "What is it? Is everything okay?" Travis squinted with intrigue.

"Don't worry my love, it's okay." Jenny whispered as she made her way out of the clinic.

The sun was setting low on the horizon. There was such sweetness to the twilight now. Travis walked his young wife to their car. He opened the door for her as he always did and shut her in. He seemed a little perplexed at Jenny's visible difference coming out of the clinic. She seemed very different, sparkling different. The strain of the situation seemed to be less intense now.

Travis jumped in the car and looked at Jenny. She was so beautifully serene sitting there. It was not her usual forced smiles and stressed face. She stared at him as if it were the first time they had seen each in a long time. She smiled and peered into his eyes as he looked also intently at her. Something transferred to him as he tried to really discern her. "You didn't go through with it, with the abortion, did you Jenny?"

Jenny smiled. She was so at peace. Such tranquility invaded her heart and mind. It was as if the whole world had suddenly changed.

"No Travis. Thank God, I didn't. Thank God!"

Travis visibly lit up as if an unbearable weight he had been carrying suddenly lifted. But he was somewhat perplexed as well. Jenny never spoke of God unless it was something irreligious or irreverent.

"Jenny, you are going to have to tell me what's going on? What happened to you in there? Why did it take so long, only for you to come out still pregnant? I thought that you wanted to do this with all your heart."

Jenny looked out the window as a fresh snow began to fall. She smiled and hugged her own belly.

"Let's go home. We will talk there."

On the way home Travis kept looking over at his young wife. Normally, Jenny always looked stressed and distracted about many things. But she was very relaxed now and there was a genuine smile and peaceful expression on her face. Travis turned on the headlights as it was now getting dark.

"Honey, maybe we should take you to see another doctor or something?" Travis worried out loud, also trying to fish for more intel.

"No my love, really. I'm okay. I'm actually better than I've been in a very, very long time."

"Yes Jenny, you seem very different."

"I am very different, Travis. I am now 100% a different person then the one that walked into that clinic." Jenny smiled serenely.

"By your expressions and composure... and coming from my background, honey... It sort of looks like you had some sort of born again experience in that clinic or something." Travis unknowingly quipped. Jenny genuinely laughed. "That's it exactly... sort of... I had a born again experience... or I will have one when our babies are born... again into this world!"

"Jen, you're freaking me out... what are you talking about? And why did you say babies?"

Jenny laughed again and looked into Travis's eyes. He was a good man. She loved him so much. "Travis, I am pregnant with twins."

"Twins! Really! Did the doctor discover that? Is that the reason you didn't go through with it?"

"No Travis, my babies spoke to me while I was unconscious from a bad sedative reaction. They spoke a wonderful thing to me. When I was about to speak death into them... they spoke life into me! They spoke to me about my right to choose life!" Jenny's tears trickled down her face now.

I'm pro-choice about being pro-life now!" Jenny giggled at her newfound epiphany.

"I don't understand Jen. You have been so radical and obstinate in your views about abortion and a woman's right to choose. How can you so quickly change your mind? Don't tell me that some of the things I've been telling you have finally rubbed off?" Travis was delighted that Jenny had just spoken as she had.

Jenny grabbed Travis's right hand from the steering wheel and kissed it. "Yes, my scraggly faced man... I know it might seem miraculous to you. But many of your past arguments did sink into this thick skull of mine and somehow today... they found their way to my heart."

Jenny looked penetratingly into his eyes. "Thank you my dear husband. Thank you for your words of life. Thank you for speaking your mind even when you knew I would become enraged and unbearable." Jenny kissed him again with her tears splashing the back of his hand.

"So we are keeping the baby then... or babies? Are you sure you are carrying twins?" Travis smiled and shook his head with excitement.

"We're keeping them and yes, I'm sure of it, a beautiful baby girl and boy!" Jenny hugged her belly again.

Travis's eyes sparkled now. "Two for the price of one!"

Jenny could really tell that he had never wanted the abortion at all. He had merely gone along with the abortion for her.

"So if it's a girl and a boy, I guess we'll need to come up with some names for them then." Travis muttered out loud.

"I already know their names but what would you name them?" Jenny asked playfully and curiously.

"Oh, I don't know about a girl's name but I've always entertained the idea to name a future son after my grandfather Kenneth."

Jenny giggled and declared. "And so he will be... He will be Kenneth!"

There was a long silence in the car as they both pondered the implications of their new reality. Finally Travis broke the quiet. "So you know it's going to be a lot harder. We're going to have to adjust our current lifestyles and school schedules a whole bunch, right?" Travis sighed with the reality sinking in.

"Yes. I know. But no matter what adjustments we have to make or the hardships... I already know it will be worth it. Anything we go through, it will be worth it. Life is always worth it. The blessing always outweighs the burden." Jenny peacefully pondered out loud.

"Uh Oh! So what about your responsibilities and activities with your Pro-Choice group?" Travis inquired.

"I am going to still be active... only I will just be on the other side of the road with my picket sign!" Jenny smiled and winked. "Besides, I think I am also going to change my major to journalism. I've always liked to write. Also, I think we should take your Dad up on his offer to attend his church."

Travis choked up and shook his head in so much disbelief. Is this the same woman who used to be so strongly opposed to anything religious and vehemently defended her radical left ideas? Sure, Travis had sometimes prayed for his headstrong wife but he didn't really think God was listening... since he himself had strayed so far from the path.

Travis spoke with a silly southern drawl. "Lordy, Lordy, God have mercy! Miracles will never cease! Some great glorious thing has truly taken place at that clinic! Are you sure you're alright little lady?"

Jenny laughed. "Yes, I'm sure I am okay." Jenny shined.

Jenny gazed down toward the middle of the car's interior at the little compartment that was folded down between the front seats. She noticed something peculiar that caught her eye. She reached for the small moist object. "What is this?" She barely uttered.

Jenny examined a mostly eaten gala apple with only the core remaining. It had a couple seeds hanging on the inside of the core that were slightly sprouting already. Then like a flash, she remembered. The nurse had instructed her to not eat anything before the abortion procedure. Jenny had cheated by eating the apple on the way to the clinic before she was to have the procedure performed. She remembered seeing the seeds while eating the apple and thinking about them. She actually had a passing thought that the seeds were mystically trying to tell her something even then. But she quickly dismissed the thoughts as self made, paranoid conjectures due to her apprehension and nervousness before the procedure. Jenny marveled within herself at how God had worked the apple seeds into her life changing experience. Travis was also marveling at his wife's sudden new disposition as they neared their humble little farmhouse.

The Beginning

Travis and Jenny pulled up into their driveway with the headlights beaming on the little hillside next to the rickety farmhouse. Travis turned off the headlights. Jenny's eyes widened at the sight of the wood worn farmhouse. She loved it now more than ever before. Jenny's eyes turned and became fixed on the hillside landscape before her.

Jenny pointed at the hillside, deep in thought.

"What? What?" Travis sputtered.

Jenny got out of the car still transfixed on the hillside. Travis also got out and walked over to Jenny's side, trying to discern why she took such a sudden interest in the snowy landscape.

"Love, come with me." Jenny grabbed Travis by the hand and began to lead him to the little hillside.

As they tromped through the snow, Travis wondered if Jenny had lost her mind. Jenny looked at Travis with such a joyous bliss and excitement on her face. She began to relate her experience when she was passed out on the clinic surgery table. She spoke so fast that Travis had to slow her down several times. She told him of how she had seen her own frozen corpse in the snow and the detectives talking about her suicide... then the memories of the snowball fights, the twins growing up, the tradition of the snow angel family, Mr.& Mrs. Apple Tree, the nightmare abortions she had and then her rich, successful but lonely life without her family. Jenny told Travis how beautiful their little family was... about Kaley & Kenny. She told him everything through broken, joyous tears mixed with spurts of genuine giggles. Travis stood their stunned and amazed at her story.

He too began to show emotion.

"I want our family to be like that... just like that, Jenny. I've always dreamed of a family like that with you... I just never thought it would ever..."

"I know Travis and now you have one, my love, now you have one!" Jenny's tears of joy froze on her face.

"Thank you God!" Jenny and Travis both shouted almost in unison. They held hands and twirled in the snow. They danced like little children. They were truly on fire with sudden happiness. Travis was so excited. His anxiety and guilt ridden conscience dissolved in the snow speckled wind. He had always wished for Jenny to be the kind of woman that wanted to raise children and have a family. He could see that Jenny had so genuinely, miraculously changed. Her eyes were beaming with joy now. Jenny pulled Travis close and pointed to the browning apple core still in her hand.

"We can cultivate these apple seed sprouts now and in late spring, near the delivery of our twins, we will transfer them to right here on the top of this hill, overshadowing the slope just like in my dream of Kenny and Kaley." Jenny outshined the moon now peeking out in the winter draped night.

"Sure, Jenny we will!"

Jenny pecked Travis's cheek playfully and then plopped herself on the snow covered hillside. She motioned Travis to lay next to her. Travis complied.

Jenny began to flap her arms and legs. Travis followed suit. They both made snow angels and laughed at themselves lying in the snow. Jenny laughed so genuinely. They both got up almost at the same time to look at their snow angels.

"Now we have our first snow angel family and a start of a good tradition!" Jenny blurted.

"I'm so happy that you changed your mind, Jenny. I am really happy that we are going to have the babies and be a family! This is the best Christmas gift ever!"

Jenny remembered the similar conversation with her children in the dream.

"Yes, you are right Travis... our children, Kaley and Kenny Daniels... they are the best Christmas gift ever!" Jenny burst out with glee.

Travis grabbed his young pregnant wife and whisked her off her feet. He carried her to a large pine all covered in snow that grew near their front porch. He set her on her feet and looked deep into her eyes.

"I have always loved you Jenny. But I'd been struggling with this whole thing so very much. And I know we have fought a lot lately. I was really afraid that our lives were starting to radically go down different paths... that I was losing you. I even prayed to God that you might change your mind. Now, I feel as if God answered my prayer but better than I could have ever imagined! Jenny, I love you so much and I feel our lives together just made a turn towards a most wonderful, beautiful, scenic route!"

Travis grabbed her face with both his hands and kissed her. Jenny looked up into his brown eyes and smiled. She was truly so happy with her total reversal of everything she had once believed. She felt good, wholesome and a sense of rightness that went beyond just a change in perspectives. It was truly a heart transformation, a spiritual cleansing, a metamorphosis. Jenny kissed him back.

Travis suddenly whisked her again and carried her to the front porch of the old rickety house. He stood her up again. They both stood silent and breathed in the moment. Travis opened the front door and walked in.

"Let me get a fire going for our brand new little family!" He sparked. Jenny lingered a bit longer, having stepped off the front porch onto the yard again. She suddenly thought she heard an echo of when Travis had whispered in her ear in the dream. In the light, snow speckled wind she heard within her soul, "The measure of God's mercy goes far beyond the measure of our sins, Jenny."

She looked over at where Mr. & Mrs. Apple Tree would one day stand overshadowing her snow angels. "Thank you again God for your mercy and giving me a first time, second chance." Jenny prayed. She looked at the angelic impressions one last time before she went in. "And thank you for my Kaley and my Kenny, for they really are my angels in the snow!"

"Jen, come in from the cold and let's get warmed up!" Travis beckoned from the door.

"I have already come in from the cold... and I am already so very warmed, my love!" Jenny replied, still lingering outside. She blew a kiss towards heaven with both her hands and twirled in a victory pose as the snow fell softly all around her. Jenny hugged her belly twice and walked inside her humble little home to be with Travis, the father of her beautiful twins.

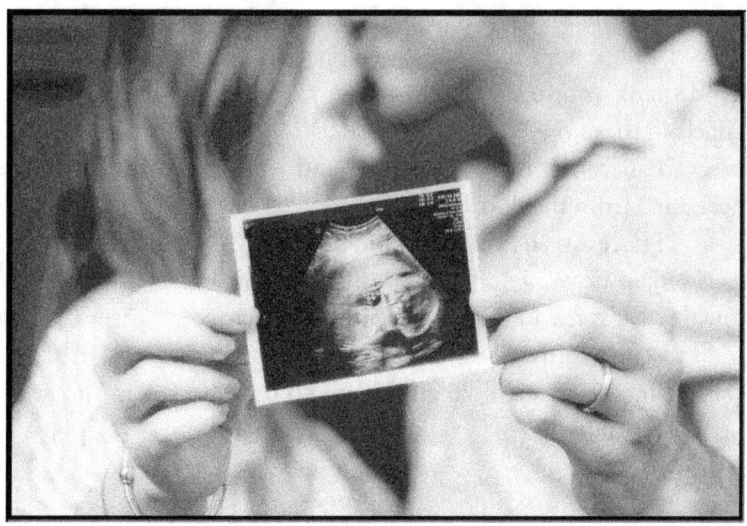

A Brand Plucked Out Of The Fire

"If I can stop one heart from breaking, I shall not live in vain. If I can ease one life the aching, Or cool one pain, Or help one fainting robin Unto his nest again, I shall not live in vain."
~Emily Dickinson

Yes, "Angels In The Snow" may seem to be a bit of fiction but the truth is, when Father God Almighty pierces every shadow within the hearts of men on that day, how many mothers and fathers will see the alternate reality or time line that "could have been" for the children they unfortunately gave up?

How many of them will see what Jenny saw, a love and laughter that only haunts them in their childless reality? How many will one day weep in anguish and sorrow to regret the decision to abort their precious babies? How many will see that if they had decided to keep their children it would have given them a whole new life of purpose and destiny?

"Angels In The Snow" may not be based on a true story but it was inspired by true events. You see, let me briefly tell you a true story of my life, as "a brand plucked out of the fire."

Many people have never heard this part of my life but yes... I am a little passionate and radical about the abortion issue. Not because I have just an academic or moral grasp on the subject but more importantly because I myself, am a survivor of an attempted abortion.

It was 1967 and hippies were all about peace, love and sexual freedom... and oh yea, broken homes, deadbeat dads and single mothers... single mothers trying to raise their children in between the half smoked marijuana joint in the ashtray and the empty beer cans lying on the psychedelic shag carpet.

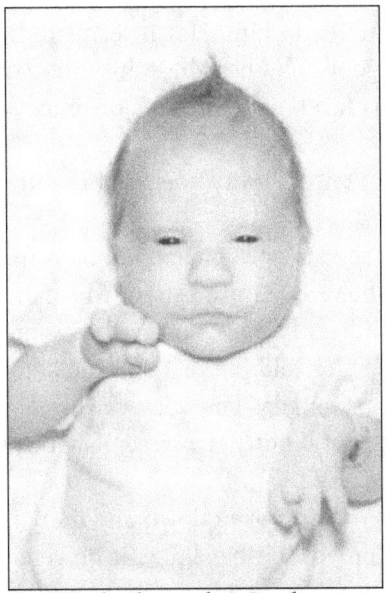

Heath Christopher Goodman
Showing Off My Designer Fingers

The doctor looked grimly at the young mother who had just given birth to her now third child. "I am sorry to have to inform you Mrs. Goodman but the birth of your son Heath, was not without complications. It seems that Heath has been born with multiple birth defects. I am afraid he will have some permanent deformities."

"What do mean birth defects? Deformities?" Sandra's heart sank as she thought of the worst things possible. "What is it? Is he okay? Is it his head or face? Is he missing legs or arms?"

"No, Mrs. Goodman, the good news is that it is limited defects and marginal deformities. Your son was born with some birth defects to his hands. He is missing a couple fingers and others did not develop normally. His feet are turned in, or what is known as clubfoot."

"Will Heath be alright? Will he be able to walk?"

"Yes, clubfoot is a more common birth defect. With casts and proper medical care, we should be able to correct his feet."

Sandra began to cry from the emotion of it. "Doctor, is my baby going to be alright?"

The doctor sat down to Sandra's eye level to comfort her. "We have done extensive tests on him. Heath seems to be a healthy baby otherwise. He has a good solid heartbeat, his internal structures seem to be normal and his head, torso and major limbs seem to be up to stat."

"Please doctor, tell me why was he born this way?" Sandra sniffled.

The doctor grabbed the pen on his clipboard and looked intently at Sandra. "Sandy, you've been my patient for many years now. I've treated all of your children. I know you have had some very hard times in your life. You have also told me that you did smoke and consume alcohol during your pregnancy. Did you ever use any other drugs or take any medications that I didn't prescribe that you are not telling me about?"

Sandra hesitated. She looked down and away from the doctor's gaze. Sandra teared up and bit her lip as it quivered uncontrollably. "Well, Doctor, there was one incident that I have been too ashamed to mention to you. I was so depressed and so distraught about my marriage and my life. I did something when I had been drinking and not right in my mind... Something that I now regret..." Sandra's tears choked her up and she couldn't finish her statement.

The doctor sat staring at her to complete her sentence.

"Some friends of mine told me that if I took a certain amount of these pain pills that it would induce a miscarriage and I could terminate my pregnancy. So one night after I had been drinking very heavily, I wasn't thinking straight and my emotions got the best of me. I took a bunch of pain pills to try to abort my child." Sandra was sobbing now.

"I woke up the next morning regretting what I had done... I realized I had failed the attempt... and I really wanted my baby... but oh doctor, do you think what I did might have caused Heath's birth defects?"

"Ahh, well, maybe... We don't really know. Many factors could have contributed to it, Sandra. But the main thing now is, he seems to be in good health. He will grow up with some stigma and handicaps. We will monitor his deformities and the extent of his detriments. However, you must move forward to be a good mother to him just as you have been with your other two children."

Marked from my birth with these front and center deformities, I would soon surrender my disenfranchised boyhood to a state of oddity and negative curiosity. On top of this, I grew up in a turbulent, godless family environment with so much drugs, alcohol, dysfunction and despair. My parents divorced early on and my brother and I were torn between two worlds... and both of them were "Helter Skelter scary" and uncertain.

As I entered my school years, I was bullied and ridiculed by other kids for my birth defects. I was consistently made fun of and looked down upon by my peers. I felt inferior. A freak of nature, ashamed of who I was... or, what I was. In school and with my other siblings and cousins, I longed to be a "normal" person. To have friends, to be popular, to have girls like me. To be an equal with other children. Instead I was teased and called "Funny Fingers" and "Nubs".

I remember times coming home from school so sad and lonely for friendship. I experienced what no child should... the faces of other children looking at me with disgust and contempt for something totally out of my control. The kids who bullied me knew I would not fight back because I was already beaten up on the inside. I was more traumatized than the girls who physically recoiled in horror if I even accidentally brushed by them in passing. Sometimes I even felt inhuman. There were many times I was left out of the children's games during recess. No one wanted to play with the boy with deformed fingers. During P.E. I was always the one player picked last or the odd man left out.

But more than anyone else, I began to dislike who I was on the inside.

With a very physically and verbally abusive father, my seed of self loathing seemed to be compounded with a sense of worthlessness. As a boy with an overactive imagination at times, I remember I entertained the idea that I was some sort of alien from outer space. I used to get my kid brother to believe it anyway. If I was not of this world, it would explain a lot. I liked this grand explanation of intrigue and fascination rather than my reality based, battered, broken, glaringly deformed state of being. Star Trek made it a possibility but unfortunately, I kept getting slapped in the face with the reality that I was just a boy with odd shaped fingers.

As an adolescent, I actually became somewhat extroverted. I thought that since everyone else saw me as the butt of a joke and a good laugh that maybe I should join them. Thus I developed into a troublesome class clown. You see, I figured the best way to deal with the hurtful sneers and jeers was to turn them into a desired response. In my little boy brain, I figured that if I did or said anything silly, I could control the laughter... so it wouldn't directly hurt me anymore. It worked sometimes.

So when anyone laughed at me, I laughed with them. Of course, the teachers at school didn't think I was that funny as I interrupted their sacred teaching moments with my wit and humor. They didn't stop to smell the roses... so I was regularly "in trouble" at the principle's office.

Growing up into a very troubled young man, my disposition gradually flip flopped as I became a drug and alcohol user. Becoming a regular marijuana smoking hippy and a drug and alcohol crazed youth at age 12, I liked how those substances seemed to make me feel... more human, more confident to interact with people. It lowered my inhibitions of self doubt, self hatred and beaten down persona.

Drugs and alcohol desensitized my inner pain and rejection. They made me feel complete, equal, even like I had a magical transformation when using... from a bumbling, freakish ogre to a suave "Indiana Jones". Although, the truth was these chemicals just inflated my injured ego while dumbing me down to that of a 5 year old... a common effect on all who partake in the communion of stupid juice (alcohol) and stupid smoke (marijuana).

However, without these substances, I felt even more pathetic and downtrodden.

My isolation and rejection in junior high and high school turned me somewhat into a reclusive soul. Yes, I was the guy who ate at the school lunch table all by himself. I was the student who missed more classes then I attended. I was just a hair away from dropping out of school altogether.

You see, I was the sole "long haired hippy dude" among the rednecks, jocks, nerds and social snobs of the small podunk school in Texas. Back then, "hippy folks" were not so well received in rural redneck America. My deformities only compounded the problem.

On one occasion, I remember a very popular jock with his attractive girlfriend. As they passed by me one day, both of them looked at me and my hands with such disdain. The jock ridiculed me in front of his girlfriend. He yelled out "Finger Freak" and smirked. I immediately held out my hands for them to take a real good look. "Hey, you have front row tickets to see the freak!" I shouted at them. It was the only time I can remember I tried to confront and shame my scorners head on. Most of the time I just took the bitter pill... along with the marijuana and beer that made it much easier to swallow.

I began to drink more and more, smoke more pot and do harder drugs into my teenage years. I also retreated into sci-fi novels and fantasy books. Inwardly, I grew morose, depressed and very resentful. I was already spiraling furiously downward at the early age of 15.

However, when I was a few months away from my sixteenth birthday, an amazing transformation happened to me. I saw my life heading towards Nowhereville and off the cliffs of Insanity.

I called on God for help and suddenly like a whirlwind, I became "one of those meddling, born again Christians". I immediately quit smoking and had no more obsession for drugs and alcohol. In literally the blink of an eye, I had a personal spiritual awakening and "moral metamorphosis."

With God, my psyche and soul began a slow healing. I began to make friends at school and I no longer ate alone at lunch time.

I remember that my whole perspective changed. For the first time, I noticed beautiful trees and flowers and recognized my Creator's handiwork. It was if I had been living all my life in a cold, dark cellar and someone suddenly catapulted me into the big blue, sun shiny sky.

I also started to enjoy writing after this. I started to write poetry and prose. I liked to reflect the solitude of my thoughts on paper. Unbeknown at that time to my own abortion survival, I remember that for some reason (during the Reagan years) I began growing a conscience towards the abortion issue. One of the first real poems I ever wrote which I later turned into a song was on the subject of abortion. It seemed a little "radical" at the time but I think it's probably not radical enough these days.

I AM THE CHILD *(The Little Martyr's Song)*

Hello, I am the child
Whose deathbed is my own mother's womb.
My life becomes a shattered dream
As I partake in Abel's doom.
Hello, I am the infant
Whose destiny is a plastic bag grave.
And my epitaph reads,
"Crushed hopes of an unknown babe!"
I have no rights so I have no choice... but to die.
I can not protest without a voice...
Won't you be my cry?
I need your tears to plead my cause... I want to be!
If you don't care to change the laws...
you've helped murder me!

Hello, I am the baby
Who lives only to be put to death.
And in my dying gasp,
I take my first breath.
Hello, I am the little one
Whose faith is in my very life.
But before my faith becomes sight
I meet up with the doctor's knife!

Good-bye, I was the child
Put to death by my own parent's hands.
Oh, my blood cries out for justice!
Who for me, will take a stand?
Good-bye, I was the baby
Whose soul was never seen in flesh and bone.
Though men destroy this earthly house,
They can never touch my eternal home!
I am cut off before I bloom. Embryo is my name?
A tissue mass in bottled glass? My coffin on display!
Can you hear my silent cry, "I want to be!"
I wave hello just to say good-bye.
My life unknown to me.

My father passed away soon after my conversion. I somehow inherited a large folder of his old personal correspondences to my mother and their divorce lawyers. It also contained personal letters, and the legal documents from their custody battle for myself and my brother.

I never remembered my parents ever being together. Though they were flagrant, self absorbed hippies, I was curious about why they divorced. So I began reading the letters and documents. I learned some fascinating but also disturbing things about my mother and father.

I stumbled onto something that disturbed me very much in particular. A surprising explanation to why I was born with multiple deformities. It seemed to bring into focus my whole childhood identity crisis and real closure to much of my teenage years of hurt and rejection.

I read a letter my father wrote to his lawyer giving an eye opening account of my mother. How one night in a drunken depression during her pregnancy with me, she attempted to abort me by taking an overdose of pain pills. He went on to tell the lawyer that he had doctors confirm that this could very well be why I was born with multiple birth defects. It was at the very crucial time that as a fetus, my hands and feet were developing when my mother had taken the overdose.

However, I was only a little upset that I had never been told this by my mother. As a Christian now, I also knew that it was her shame and regret that kept her from telling me about it.

But I did confront my mother. Not in some unforgiving way, but more as a friend to a friend. She confessed and wept to speak of it. I loved my mother and forgave her instantly without a hint of rage or resentment.

My mother had become a beautiful soul and we had a great relationship. I knew that she had some very turbulent moments in her past. But since that revelation of the attempted abortion, I came to realize that my own redemption story has had hidden layers to it.

Now, since my mother did in fact attempt to abort me, I can be rightly defined as "a brand plucked out of the fire", that is, an "abortion survivor." I may not be anything of importance to this world in other matters but I know I can advocate the rights of the unborn with both conviction and a true sense of a crusader's voice, one born out of such adversity.

If my birth defects were related to my mother's terrible decision to try to abort me, which is highly probable, then I think I can say that I held on for dear life and have the battle scars to prove it! My commitment to life and the cause of the unborn began with my own survival. I have every right to stand on a platform and cry out in defense of those of my fallen comrades who were not and are not as fortunate as I. I weep to think of this age where countless millions of beautiful, precious babies have been slaughtered without shame or remorse. I must be a voice for them since I have shared in their suffering.

This is why I wrote "Angels In The Snow."

I have felt a heavy conviction of guilt for years for staying so silent on the subject, for not crying out against the horror and injustice of abortion. Even my mother became more of a crusader to the issue than I. I have a large collection of scrap articles, petitions, and advertisements that my mother had so meticulously kept when she was alive. I remember on several occasions when she would literally start to weep when we got on the subject of abortion. One time I recall her saying in her passionate tears, "Heathy, why can't they see that they're just little babies? They are just little precious babies!" I remember those wailing words piercing my own heart to become more of an advocate.

Now my conscience has grown unbearable as the statistics continue to rise and the lives of untold millions of unborn children are cruelly cut off from their God given right to life.

Now that a new wave of militant leaders are poised to proliferate the carnage and set more murderous lawlessness into motion, A cry must go out against the bloody tide.

Yet I cry out not as loud as the blood of these precious martyrs whose voices quake from the very ground! None of us are guiltless if we remain neutral or silent as the slaughter continues! We can not be on the sidelines of this holocaust.

The Holy Scriptures declare that it is our responsibility to defend the defenseless, to protect the innocent. Yes, God has mandated us to be His hands, His feet, His voice, the conveyor of His righteousness. Yes, we are to live out what we say we believe. Imagine that!

Here are just a few scriptures in the Word of God that shows that without exception, we are all called to get involved to save precious babies, to get on the Pro-Life bandwagon-

"Rescue those who are being taken away to death; hold back those who are stumbling to the slaughter. If you say, "Behold, we did not know this," does not He who weighs the heart perceive it? Does not He who keeps watch over your soul know it, and will He not repay man according to his work?" Proverbs 24:11-12

"So it is not the will of my Father who is in heaven that one of these little ones should perish." Matthew 18:14

"Open your mouth for the mute, for the rights of all who are destitute. Open your mouth, judge righteously, defend the rights of the poor and needy." Proverbs 31:8-9

"Give justice to the weak and the fatherless; maintain the right of the afflicted and the destitute. Rescue the weak and the needy; deliver them from the hand of the wicked." Psalm 82:3-4

"*Wash yourselves, make yourselves clean; Put away the evil of your doings from before My eyes. Cease to do evil, Learn to do good; Seek justice, Rebuke the oppressor; Defend the fatherless, Plead for the widow.*" Isaiah 1:17

"*Thus says the Lord: Do justice and righteousness, and deliver from the hand of the oppressor him who has been robbed. And do no wrong or violence to the resident alien, the fatherless, and the widow, nor shed innocent blood in this place.*" Jeremiah 22:3

Not For The Faint Of Heart

They say the pen is mightier than the sword. I hope this is true for I write now with passionate force and a great obsession to somehow make a difference. I pray perhaps the flow of this ink could in some way stop the flow of blood from the sword which slays the most innocent and vulnerable among us- the unborn, unwanted children of this wayward, broken world! Yes, "Angels In The Snow" was designed to be a good story to delicately marinate the consciences of readers in Pro-Life perspectives, to tenderize them to the true nature of what abortion really is- the snuffing out of precious life and the destinies of countless millions on this earth.

However, I must lovingly give a disclaimer that the next few pages are designed to be more like a meat grinder to completely tenderize the hardened consciences of those of us who have been demoralized and desensitized by an ever increasingly wicked, self centered, godless society.

Unfortunately, many of us have had a myriad of hands who have clawed and torn apart the very face of our God-given consciences until our hearts and minds have unknowingly been plundered and disfigured... to the point that most of us don't even realize how far we have wandered off path or from whence we have fallen.

We "can't see the forest because of the trees." We have grown up around such decadence and apostasy (the forest) that we can't see how grossly perverse and out of whack our culture and subsequent compromised Christianity (the trees) has become. We think it's "normal" and "quite alright" to munch on popcorn and gulp down a Coke while unflinchingly watch the most bloody violent scenes of innocent people getting gunned downed and massacred as part of our entertainment for an evening.

We don't realize how barbaric and psychopathic/sociopathic these things really are. Hollywood has gradually pulled us into such compromise and corruption of the soul. It's all just "pretend" and so we watch on... not realizing that the "entertainment" has *entered* our souls. We *retain* the residual shock and awe until it gradually hardens our hearts and deadens our consciences. Then when it is not "pretend" massacres and bloodshed, we are not so pierced, so convicted and alarmingly seized with motivation and effort to do anything about it.

We have become cold and callous spectators in a bread and circus crowd. As long as it doesn't directly affect me, myself and I or "us four and no more", then we nonchalantly and apathetically live out our lives, unbeknown of how frozen and loveless our hearts have become. One of the most often overlooked signs of the end of days that Jesus mentioned was, *"And because lawlessness will be increased, the love of many will grow cold." Matthew 24:12*

No, none of us like to have our consciences flogged and "smitten" as truth often stings really bad. Truth often is a painful recalibration of the soul. We cringe to be under the extreme brilliant light of truth and the fire of God's holiness... but if we will submit to the process, desensitization, deception and darkness can be purged out of us. We need our hearts and consciences to be examined, exposed and exfoliated with the divine, moral absolutes of God.

Unfortunately, many people in this generation seem to be of a very hyper-sensitive and fragile disposition who can't even take the slightest correction or rebuke without it being transformed into a tsunami of rejection, "bullying" or "bigoted shaming". Some are so feeble that they almost literally curl up into a fetal position if you happen to tell them one of their shoes is untied. They are constantly

78

offended and can not endure being exposed and brought into the light. A person has to walk on eggshells around them for fear of a meltdown.

I think this frail mentality is one of the greatest indictments against a generation who only seek acceptance and positive affirmation no matter how they act or think. The more we reject correction and instruction, the weaker we become.

No one wants to feel shame or guilt for anything anymore. Yet the Bible says, *"A fool despises his father's instruction, But he who receives correction is prudent."* **Proverbs 15:5** Many more scriptures speak of how correction and rebuke is necessary and brings wisdom, understanding and peace to those who receive it.

Only fools despise correction (as they pride themselves as "free-spirited" and "controlled by no law or restraints") and continue down the path of disorder and eventual destruction. But those who want to continually improve themselves towards good character, virtue and integrity, then correction and rebuke is actually invited and accepted as a way of life. *"For the commandment is a lamp; and the law is light; and reproofs of instruction are the way of life."* **Proverbs 6:23** *"Better is open rebuke than hidden love."* **Proverbs 27:5**

So this being said, it is my intention as lovingly as possible to share God's Word and the correction and rebuke it offers to all of us. However, many times no matter how gentle and kind we attempt to be, truth will often be taken as harsh and abrasive to the insolent, unbroken, brazenly foolish and wicked.

Darkness hates the light and recoils in contempt, accusatory rhetoric and hyped up fake rage to detract from being exposed. Evil by its own nature does not want to be under the scrutiny of discerning eyes. Neither does it want to be outed as fraudulent and without substance.

Jesus was very loving and gentle with the humble and broken. For they were ready to receive correction to change their lives for the better. However, in contrast Jesus was also very loving yet abrasive with the proud and rebellious. "Woe to you, hypocrites!" This is because it is more loving to try to break the hardness of someone's heart with truth that is harder than that heart. Without a hammer of truth or a fire of passionate confrontation, the deceived soul can never be jolted into reality or hopefully broken to see the error of their ways. *"Is not my word like fire, declares the LORD, and like a hammer that breaks the rock in pieces?" Jeremiah 23:29* Hard rocks can only be broken or cut by a harder substance. If we don't humbly submit ourselves to being broken by truth, unfortunately, in the end, truth will still win over our pride and rebellion but instead, we will broken without remedy. This is why Jesus made the somewhat cryptic statement, *"And whoever falls on this stone will be broken; but on whomever it falls, it will grind him to powder." Matthew 21:44 "He who is often rebuked, and hardens his neck, will suddenly be destroyed, and that without remedy." Proverbs 29:1* It only makes sense that if we don't receive correction and reproof concerning the right ways of God, then there is nothing left but to receive judgment. Correction is the mercy God wants to bring to us instead of His judgment.

Unfortunately, in this day, it is no longer a time to speak softly and gently to a callous, impudent generation who equate unborn children as a malignant cancer or an infected boil to be happily excised from the body. It is not a time to marginalize or sanitize the brutal slaying of countless millions of babies. Nor is it a time to bow down to "political correctness". Nor should we cower to a "dampened and dumbed down" form of Christianity that has lost it's fear of God and it's prophetic voice, "crying in the wilderness to make straight paths for the Lord".

For every church leader who is unwilling to speak boldly against abortion for fear of worldly persecution, retribution or loss of livelihood, I challenge them to truly get a backbone and quit being some sort of a "jellyfish, half-hearted believer" and to genuinely seek to know the holy, awesome God they claim to follow.

Jesus was not a namby pamby Messiah. He overturned the tables of the money changer's and drove them out of the temple with whips. The zeal of the Lord and His house consumed Him. So likewise, how much more should the zeal of God consume us to be the voice of these innocent babies being mercilessly slaughtered solely out of the pure selfishness and hedonism of this lawless generation?

Deep down inside, everyone of us knows that abortion is the taking of innocent life. There is no real debate. Science and common sense clearly confirms this. It's literally hardwired into our consciences even if half the population has seared their conscience with a hot iron of psychobabble and junk science. Liberal indoctrination or to claim "ignorance" will not hold up under the light of God's eye. He will not give you a free pass because you decided to just regurgitate godless ideology and did not stop to think it all the way through.

It's really not an issue that we should academically or intellectually argue upon political platforms to give any credence to those who support it. Just as how ridiculous it would be to debate whether or not the sky is blue or the grass is green. Though it has become a hotbed "controversy" for the bread and circus media, where celebrities and political figures want to show support for or exercise their right to kill the unborn, we should give them no spotlight or soapbox to encourage such murderous agendas. Just as we would never give serial killers a microphone on primetime television to express justifications for their heinous crimes against humanity.

Sadly, the airwaves are dominated by the left and the hoards of demons who are ruled by the "prince of the air". Yet in a world set aright, there is nothing to debate when it comes to obvious immoral and depraved actions and behaviors.

The only reason abortion is even "an issue" today is because somewhere in the past we capitulated to faulty moral ambiguity, hedonistic logic and reasoning. Somewhere we compromised common sense and righteous conviction for a delusion of lawlessness.

Once we made it legal, that is, legitimized abortion, it's almost impossible to backtrack and bring the moral hammer back down on a people who have loved the freedom to casually but brutally throw away their children.

However, It's my intent to set your heart and mind on fire, to be more than just a nonchalant dissenter or a mere spectator among those who volley the abortion "debate". I wish your heart to be instead a blazing inferno of zeal and truth to boldly defend those who can't defend themselves. I pray for the kindling to begin even now!

A fire rages within me which sorely burns my waking conscience and brings tears of anguish to my soul as I must constantly make public consumption of this perverse and twisted generation and the murderous, bloody ideology of "Pro-Choice". Surely persons with even half of a soul can see the blatant truth, to burn down the rotting, maggot filled social constructs of a generation who think murdering babies is the most humane way to implement birth control? Or that killing unwanted, innocent infants is how we solve the consequential ramifications of rampant promiscuity and marital unfaithfulness in this decadent society?

Yes, Virginia, it would be better if men and women readily submitted to chemical castration or sterilization than to kill precious babies. In this advanced age of technology, it would be more humane to demand or mandate promiscuous people to use contraceptives, or become sterile (even temporarily) than to continue injecting deadly poisons into the skull of precious babies and ripping them limb by limb to remove their body parts from the womb.

Most Christians and traditional moralists are not opposed to the very cheap and affordable ways of birth control as long as conception has not taken place. Some contraceptives are actually designed to kill a baby upon it's conception. Why don't we strengthen technologies and laws to enforce preventative solutions rather than the killing of unborn infants? It's actually cheaper and "look Ma, no blood on my hands!"

The unadulterated fact remains that the current holocaust of slaughtering our precious children is no doubt, 100% because our culture has turned sex into a "must have" god with no consequences. We worship on the altar of fleshly appetites to produce a quick second euphoric, orgasmic feeling without regard to anyone but ourselves... damn the men and women we use and abuse in the process... and let's poison, butcher and kill the children who we accidentally procreate in that momentary thrill ride.

Come on! Has our reproductive organs truly become the primary driving force of self centered pleasure with no regard to moral accountability? Why is it that men and women are so pathetically consumed in one small bodily organ becoming the very existential face of who they are, wrapping their "defined happiness" and whole identity up in what their gender is or what they might fantasize it to be? You are way more than your sex organ!

Or like brute beasts, shall a mere momentary, fleshly pleasure transcend the very moral code of right and wrong divinely hardwired within our souls and our psyches?

How can we sear with a hot iron, our God given consciences to promote and proliferate lawless sexual perversion and the brutal slaying of innocent children from such behaviors? Do we really think we will stand before God Almighty justified (pure in our own eyes) in either supporting or engaging in these things? I don't know how Democrats can support abortion and say in the same breath that they're doing God's will too. Except by the scripture that says, *"There is a generation of those who are pure in their own eyes and are yet unwashed of their filth." Proverbs 30:12*

Only a totally deceived, harlot people and church system could promote murder, sexual promiscuity and perversion and call it righteous or "progressive". It is digression into barbarianism, heathenism and godlessness.

Alas, if we could truly see how holy, how righteous and how pure our Creator God really is, how His holiness is referred to as an "All Consuming Fire", where even the holiest prophets and priest fell on their faces as dead men, trembling before His awesome presence, we would surely see how disgusting, how vile and how thoroughly corrupt our own flesh and spirit is in this fallen, broken world!

Sodom and Gomorrah were turned to cities of ash forever as an example for those who live so wickedly as to put their sexual debauchery above their God given conscience of right and wrong.

But who are we really fooling? We all know deep down what is truly wholesome, just and pure.

We all know by obvious natural observation that men and women were created by God as the symbiotic vessels for procreation. The reproductive organs overwhelmingly declare their true operative design and that they were beautifully and marvelously engineered for a specific function by a wise, intelligent Creator.

We all know that anything else is truly a perversion of the creation and a total rebellion against His divine purposes. We all know that the offspring or children created by this union between a man and woman are suppose to be part of a close-knit, committed family unit.

We all know deep down that God's law and order of lifelong

marriage and family is right and truly the wholesome, social fabric of culture and society.

Just as there is no true debate whether God exists or not, there is no true debate that His holy ways are right and good.

Yet the wicked rant and rave that "God is dead" and they are not under any divine authority or law. They can have sex any way they want, debase humans as pieces of meat and kill any baby that gets in the way of their "fun" or convenience!

Those of us who know beyond a doubt that there is an intelligent Creator behind every creation in this incredible biosphere and that He is holy, pure and just, we cringe at the insolence. We shudder that fragile, mere mortals and ignorant men so defiantly set themselves above the Divine and His holy blessing and protection.

We remember Lot's wife who even though she physically escaped from the debauchery and promiscuity of those wicked cities of Sodom, she defied the Word of the Lord. She must have been one of these whose love had grown cold and indifferent. She must have loved and supported those abominable lifestyles in her heart more than the Lord God who wanted to save her from such vile and evil. She longingly looked back at Sodom only to see the judgment of sulfur and fire as it reached out and instantly crystallized her into a pillar of salt. Known only as "Lot's wife", she became an example of one of these so called "pretend believers" who perhaps did not herself engage in the sins of Sodom but she proudly supported them on her social media page. She sympathized with sexual decadence and murder and voted for those that endorsed it.

Yet God sees our hearts and if we give our support or encouragement to wicked, abominable lifestyles or murderous, merciless acts then we demonstrate clearly that we are not a lover of the true God and His holy ways. We are self deceived and so very far from Him. We are Lot's Wife, a Sodomite at heart.

In light of God's holiness and fire, our pathetic justifications for all selfishness and sin are surely consumed like the crackling, furious flames obliterating any dry stubble. Hell is perhaps in part, the holy face of God and His justice and wrath that burns up every wicked way, every wicked, unrepentant soul that tries to enter into His presence.

The righteous are purged to redemption and purity by the blood of the Lamb but the wicked are burned to damnation and forever oblivion by the wrath of the Lamb. This is a hard truth we must embrace or else we will embrace a strong delusion and believe a lie. But God will not be mocked by our belligerent, insolent rebellion or sins. Yes, He is merciful and gracious to the humble and repentant but He resists the proud, the obstinate and the unrepentant. *"God opposes the proud but gives grace to the humble." James 4:6*

Though our new modern world has changed it's definition of morality, God has never changed. *"For I am the LORD, I do not change..." Malachi 3:6 "Jesus Christ is the same yesterday, today, and forever." Hebrews 13:8*

Our current society and culture has completely forgotten or abandoned the ways of God and His holy Word of truth. As the Apostle Paul foretold about the last days, "the lawless one" is being released upon the world now "without restraint". The consensus of this secular world currently pushes every traditionally immoral sin or behavior as now permissible, progressive and even trendy in the new, open society. Lawlessness is the new hip and fashionable thing. To be cool, you must embrace wickedness as the new social norm. Celebrities cheer on the crowd in a pitiful show of godlessness.

Christ and His apostles predicted for the end of days, that many of the churches, Christian leaders, followers and religious institutions would fall away (commit apostasy) and totally be compromised and corrupted (and not even realize from whence they have fallen).

The heathen media swarms in a frenzy to broadcast the latest celebrity preacher or so called "Christian" who defects from Christianity as if their pathetic apostasy justifies the growing lawless culture. The truth is, if all mankind gets on the bandwagon to Hell, God is still right and He is just to send a fiery annihilation to "restore all things to His holy rule and reign".

Dare to say that many pastors, preachers and evangelists stay silent or say very little on exposing sexual sins and perversions, or even cry out against abortion in their churches because they are so compromised by the fear of man, the love of money and the pride of their unoffensive "seeker sensitive" godless religion. They are hirelings and wolves who devour the sheeple and deceive so many into believing that God is a squeeze toy Teddy Bear and no longer judges us for our unrepentant sins.

However, a God fearing remnant will not bow down to the image of the beast or the carnal philosophies of this world. By the grace of God, they will not remain silent or compromise the truth. You see, they fear God alone. They have nothing but contempt for this world and it's corruption. Not that they are perfect vessels or that their judgment stands on its own virtue, yet they carry the Word of the Lord and it's His message that burns deep within them. They will cry out in the streets and expose the sins of the people and lift up the truth of Christ, which is the only way men can repent and be saved. If they be abandoned by all, imprisoned, impoverished or martyred then it is the least they can sacrifice to the God who sacrificed His all for them.

The sexual revolution in America (and abroad) directly brought on the great abortion holocaust and the great sociopathic degradation of the masses. You see, you can't have lawless sex without finding a way to easily get rid of the consequences... thus murdering millions of precious babies had to become legal and trendy. But how do you do that? Well, if you do it under the name of a supposed righteous cause like "women's rights" then the bloodbath becomes not only justified, but "inspiring" and also encouraged.

The problem is that just as a serial killer feels a little less guilty or ashamed of his murders every time he kills, deadening his conscience, finally becoming cold hearted and without any feelings whatsoever, or worse getting his kicks out of it, so likewise abortion has become so prolific and women feel so entitled to it because it has been legal for so long, that this generation is now exhibiting sociopathic and psychopathic manifestations in their protest for the "right" and entitlement to kill their babies.

There are women and feminists who wear t-shirts, or have bumper stickers and protest signs which say things like, "I am so proud I had an abortion. It was fabulous!" or "It's my body, my right!" or even more profane, deranged and psychopathic statements or behaviors. Many of them even support and are passing laws to be able to kill their babies even after they're born. Some women, doctors, "professionals" and prestigious sociologists have written articles advocating killing children up to three, four and even five years old if they are deemed unwanted or undesired!

Oh, see how the slippery slope turns to a free fall into the abyss! See how a "murder-for-convenience" population can become a sociopathic, lawless society, unhinged from all moral absolutes!

The modern, post Christian (secular) world is snacking on the comfort food of marveling at our own scientific and technological advances, assuming God is dead because A.I. is alive. We presume that our grand society must fashion a culture which removes God and religion out of any equation of reality. We "love not the truth" so we must fashion and embrace lies like evolution or "aliens as our source of origin" and so God has given us over to these deceptions.

The social damage is not only prolific but downright scary as we see the erosion of common decency and humane reasoning be replaced by mad liberals foaming at the mouth with hatred towards anyone who opposes the unhinged lawlessness and bloodshed.

The persecution and criminal violence against Christians and Pro-Life groups has skyrocketed in recent years. I'm afraid it will only get worse until the madness of this society revolts in mass and churches start burning down in droves and Christians start disappearing or being martyred in huge numbers. No, it's not paranoia when you can see the snowball ever growing as it speeds down the slope towards you. The fact of an increase in religious persecution on a global scale just goes to show that the predictions of Jesus are always spot on- *"And you will be hated by all nations because of Me." Matthew 24:9*

The truth is, unless America has some sort of great revival which is very unlikely and actually not supported by scripture concerning the last days (more scriptural references to a great apostasy), the future for this nation looks truly bleak. Violent revolution seems to be the road map of those who oppose conservative and Christian values. Either way, through revival or revolution, our churches will burn one way or the other! Let's hope and pray, it's through the fires of revival. Without it and America as we know it, is finished.

But real revival will never come unless the church and it's leaders boldly and without hypocrisy preach out against the sins of this nation, the political corruption, the hypocrisy, the shallow Churchianity, the sexual perversions, the violence and bloodshed, the unholy entertainment and corruption of our youth.

Real revival will not come unless preachers preach about the judgment to come as well. God's Word must be embraced totally, not just the soft and pleasant elements. Anyone with any discernment today can see that the judgment of the nations is at hand! We need the fear of God to once again be in the land.

However, preaching to expose sin, to call men to repent or sharing about God's judgment and wrath to come doesn't seem to be the focus or agenda of very many preachers. Fluffy, feel good messages and motivational sermonettes are more palatable to the masses... and the flow of their tithes and offerings to the church coffers.

Rather, we need preaching that is catalystic and revolutionary in nature, something likened to Holy Ghost fire. Something to awaken the sleeping mass of spiritually vexed Christians out of our lukewarm zombism and into a pure, wholesome but fiery love for God and people.

Unless we corporately get a hold of God Almighty and see a turning of the godless tide, the secular and Satanic will continue to proliferate until Christians are truly the minority. After that, I'm afraid it's going to be the "opening of the fifth seal" type of scenario- "let's round up those racist and bigoted Christians who shame us for our sins and let's chop their heads off!" *"Then the Lamb broke open the fifth seal. I saw underneath the altar the souls of those who had been killed because they had proclaimed God's word and had been faithful in their witnessing." Revelation 6:9*

Sad to say, but preachers and teachers like me will be more and more ostracized and frowned upon by the end-time harlot church system. We are looked upon as uncool preachers who just want to preach "hate" and "intolerance". But am I really being "hateful and intolerant" for quoting the Bible correctly when God says He HATES sin, murder and sexual abominations?

Of course, we're not to hate sinners or sit on our high horse in bitter, hypocritical religion... but we do have the fundamental freedom and right to hate sin and immorality... and to expose it as wickedness before our holy Creator. *"Have nothing to do with the fruitless deeds of darkness, but rather expose them." Ephesians 5:11*

In fact, exposing and informing sinners of their guilty sins before the holy Lord God is an act of true love. Unless they repent they will be eternally damned and as ministers of the true gospel, we must speak these hard truths in a spirit of love.

"Instead, speaking the truth in love, we will grow to become in every respect the mature body of him who is the head, that is, Christ." Ephesians 4:15

Or am I wrong for quoting scriptures and preaching the truth that God will not tolerate murderers, sexual perverts, thieves, liars, hypocrites and that they can not enter His kingdom but will be cast into Hell?

"Do you not know that the wicked will not inherit the kingdom of God? Do not be deceived: Neither the sexually immoral, nor idolaters, nor adulterers, nor men who submit to or perform homosexual acts, nor thieves, nor the greedy, nor drunkards, nor verbal abusers, nor swindlers, will inherit the kingdom of God. And that is what some of you were. But you were washed, you were sanctified, you were justified, in the name of the Lord Jesus Christ and by the Spirit of our God." 1 Corinthians 6:9-11

Isn't it funny that the very ones that condemn the Christians as having "hate" or "intolerance" are many times actually the first to foam at the mouth with hatred against Christians and can not "tolerate" our gospel of calling men to repentance? They want to shut us up, lock us up and run us out of the public square. Who's hating who here? Who's not tolerating who here?

True peace-loving believers genuinely tolerate the wicked more than the wicked tolerate us... and again, it's not "hate" but love to warn of God's judgment against evil, sinful behaviors.

I would be considered a hero if I screamed to wake up a man who barely escaped from a burning house. It would be considered an act of love. However, should I cry aloud to compel men to turn from their sins lest they be judged with eternal damnation in the fires of Hell, I am considered a religious bigot, a racist, a 'bully" and a "hater".

The secular society and the politically correct media circus are successfully stereotyping Christians as the backward bigots of a puritanical bygone era... just as Nazi Germany did with the Jews in the 1930's. Within a decade, Germans were dancing to the jitterbug while two doors down the gas chambers were billowing out the smoke of those self same Jews. Are we next? It appears that way.

If a great awakening and unity doesn't come to the Christian population in this country, in this world, and a massive outcry to stop the immoral madness, I'm afraid we too will soon be "aborted" without shame or guilt from a lawless, murderous society gone full pagan. Full blown Christian persecution is already happening in most of the world and very soon America too will begin to be filled with the blood of martyrs.

If our pastors and church leaders can barely "peep and mutter" about the great holocaust of precious babies being systematically slaughtered to accommodate the rampant sexual promiscuity, then how will they fare when even their compromised, watered down form of Christianity is scrutinized as unacceptable and inconsistent with the avalanche of hedonism and secularism? Oh yes, they will continue to compromise until they are full partners with the demons.

Winston Churchill once quipped, "An appeaser is one who feeds a crocodile, hoping it will eat him last." So we appease, appease, appease... until we are like the appeasers who believe that if you keep on throwing steaks to a tiger, the tiger will somehow become a vegetarian? But you run out of steaks and the tiger eventually eats you. If we keep watering down the truth, somehow the people will eventually come to love the truth? No, watered down truth is no longer truth. It is deception. *"And because they loved not the truth, God sent them a strong delusion that they might believe a lie." 2Thesselonians 2:10*

I'm certain that those who compromise truth and moral conviction to get along with a growing decadent culture will one day be accomplices in killing any and all true Christians, thinking they are doing a "service for God". You see, if you ride the fence too long, you will always fall off on the wrong side.

Make America Great Again?

Don't get political, right?

Depending on whatever side of the isle you are on, the phrase "Make America Great Again" may be positive or negative. It may be to you a grand slogan which means that you want America to prosper and for the economy to be strong as Trump and most of his supporters have implied/interpreted it to mean. Or you might see it with some darker meaning such as racism, to bring back black slavery, put the gays back in their closets and make women subservient handmaidens to men again as liberals seem to interpret it to mean. The phrase itself has morphed into two very different polarizing ideologies and most people fall into one of the camps. However, the phrase itself is really not that diabolical or controversial.

As a matter of fact, both Ronald Reagan and Bill Clinton used the slogan *"Make America Great Again"* and it was never considered racist or somehow connected to bigotry or fascism then. But today the phrase can't even be brought up in a group without someone getting offended or the group exploding into factions. This is a prime example of how one little slogan has become so politicized and demonized that now it's actually almost taboo to make mention of it. Maybe you even shuttered to just read it even now.

The truth is, the mainstream media has so sensationalized many topics to turn them into "political hotbed controversies" that peace loving individuals and Christians are prone to make them taboo subjects that we dare not speak of. Sexual perversion such as homosexuality is one of those topics. Abortion is another one. I have actually heard pastors in referring to abortion or other "political hot topics" say, "Son, we don't talk about politics or get political in this church. We want to keep the peace and not rock the boat of our unity here."

Many pastors avoid them because they are worried about their 503c status with the IRS and want to maintain a neutral stand or to keep from being called out on social media (or mainstream media) and getting a backlash of negative publicity. Nobody wants to be in that frenzied spotlight when liberal media spins a hurricane in a cup and makes the poopaganda they spew into a crapstorm.

This is how the church in America has become neutered and corrupted to stay silent on so many issues that they should be shouting from the rooftops about. The demons know that if they can turn a sin or moral issue into a political debate then they can keep most hireling and harlot preachers from ever crying out against them or exposing them. This is why you never hear the majority of preachers speak out against abortion or sexual perversion anymore.

Yet no matter what has been politicized, if it's topics that are in God's Word or affects the moral and spiritual lives of people, then we have an obligation to stay the course on revealing the truth of those topics. We can not be intimidated by a whirlwind of godless fluff. We can not be silenced by cultural taboo or political correctness. Real men and women of God will never be corralled or curtailed into a pathetic, neutered corner to appease the wicked. **"The righteous are bold as a lion." Proverbs 21:8**

Shall we not cry aloud against the sins of Sodom and Gomorrah? Shall we not dissent against a culture of fleshly heathenism, rebellion and vanity? Shall we not lift up our voices in protest against sacrificing our sons and daughters on the altars of Molech, the god of comfort and convenience? Shall we not plead with our nation to end the bloodshed of the innocent and turn our hearts back to God the Father?

Do not fall for the coward's deception as he justifies his silence and unwillingness to confront evil as being some sort of virtue of reason or keeping the peace for the sake of unity. Unity without truth and justice is a unity of devils. Better to shout truth in a den full of sleeping dragons than to tiptoe quietly in a garden of tulips full of lies and deception. Dietrich Bonhoeffer, the lonely man of God who resisted the Nazi's as his spiritual duty and political statement, until his martyrdom, wrote *"Silence in the face of evil is itself evil: God will not hold us guiltless. Not to speak is to speak. Not to act is to act."*

Shadrach, Meshach and Abednego would not bow down to the political correctness of their time. Daniel would also show his defiance and dissidence against the political issues which tried to keep him from kneeling before the One True God. Queen Esther, disregarding all political correctness would confront the king even if it cost her life, "if I perish I perish". John the Baptist and Paul stood before kings and called them to repentance. Prophets, priests and apostles throughout the centuries all confronted the sins of their nations and were not afraid to become "political" ambassadors of truth, confronting kings and commanders of armies. God fearing people are bold and "love not their lives unto death". They also love not their livelihoods unto poverty should they lose their church or ministry because no one can endure sound doctrine anymore. *"For the time will come when they will not endure sound doctrine, but according to their own desires, because they have itching ears, they will heap up for themselves teachers who will tickle their ears." 2 Tim. 4:3*

As a true believer, we never compromise Godly convictions for the sake of worldly compliance or threat of death or loss. We must be willing to serve Christ above our own lives or limbs. This is why Jesus said, *"If anyone wants to come after Me, he must deny himself and take up his cross and follow Me. For whoever wants to save his life will lose it, but whoever loses his life for My sake and for the gospel will save it. What does it profit a man to gain the whole world, yet forfeit his soul? Or what can a man give in exchange for his soul? If anyone is ashamed of Me and My words in this adulterous and sinful generation, the Son of Man will also be ashamed of him when He comes in His Father's glory with the holy angels." Mark 8:34-38*

If your pastor never confronts the issues of this decadent culture and society, if you never hear him cry out against the sins of the nation or expose this perverse and wicked generation, if you never see him passionately speak up for the unborn babies being slaughtered, then it's probably time to fire your pastor and get a pastor whose truly on fire!

This is the end times! There is no time for lukewarmness and worldly distractions in our own lives or the lives of church leaders. The Lord is coming soon and His wrath is against all nations. We need to be urgent and direct in our message to the lawless and the lost.

"Cry aloud, spare not, lift up your voice like a trumpet, and show my people their transgression, and the house of Jacob their sins." Isaiah 58:1

"Blow a trumpet in Zion; sound an alarm on my holy mountain! Let all the inhabitants of the land tremble, for the day of the LORD is coming; it is near!" Joel 2:1

Bottom line, to "Make America great again" has nothing to do with peace (military might) or prosperity (economic might). America already has an abundance of money and materialism and these are only contributing to her decadence and demise. False security is making us vulnerable to sabotage and destruction. Remember, *"When they cry prosperity, peace and safety then comes sudden destruction..." 1 Thessalonians 5:3*

To make America great again has everything to do with a revival of truth, justice and purity in the land. Unfortunately, no political figure will put that front and center on their platform... no not even Trump or any other conservative leader.

However, if all Christians would get serious with God and the church would teach and preach the true Word of God to bring people to a real relationship with Jesus and His Holy Spirit, America could become great. But alas, this seems to be so far removed from reality and because of the incredible corruption in both the church and society, such hope seems impossible. Without being a fatalist, still, *"With man this is impossible, but with God all things are possible." Matthew 19:26*

I do know judgment lies at the door for the sins of our nation. Unless there is a miraculous revival and outpouring of great repentance,

I am burdened that we will eventually be destroyed as a nation. We are already seeing much devastation in economic turmoil and natural calamities. Yes, God will protect and take care of His scattered elect but as a whole we are treading on dangerous ground. God can not hold his judgment from our unrepentant nation while destroying other nations whose sins are not even as great. He is just.

Did you know that they are actually teaching pedophilia to children now in some public schools as part of the LGBTTQQIAAP (lesbian, gay, bisexual, transgender, transsexual, queer, questioning, intersex, asexual, ally, pansexual) agenda as an "alternative" lifestyle? Transgenders with molestation records are having story time with 5 year olds in our public libraries. They are doing gender reassignment surgery on little children! Some schools are now using curriculum that teaches our 5 and 6 year old sons and daughters how to "explore their sexuality", masturbate and identify their "true gender and sexual orientation"!

Without a powerful national move of God granting us repentance and stopping the bloodshed of abortion, sexual debauchery and godless politics, we can never be "great again". Forget about "political correctness". Instead embrace "spiritual correctness" which will automatically flesh out what political side you will be on.

However, we really are at the most critical moment and crossroad as a nation today. God has always and only given us two options-

"If my people, which are called by my name, shall humble themselves, and pray, and seek my face, and turn from their wicked ways; then will I hear from heaven, and will forgive their sin, and will heal their land... But if you turn away, and forsake my statutes and my commandments, which I have set before you, and shall go and serve other gods, and worship them; Then will I pluck them up by the roots out of my land which I have given them; and this house, which I have sanctified for my name, will I cast out of my sight, and will make it to be a proverb and a byword among all nations." 2 Chronicles 7:14,19-20

Slow Escalator To Hell

The hoof beats of a hundred soldiers came into Bethlehem that day. It was the darkest moment of the inspiring Christmas story of the birth of Jesus, the savior of the world. A king had been threatened by this newborn Messiah, heir to the throne of the true kingdom of God.

But if Herod had been spiritually in tune, he would have known that such a baby was no real threat to his earthly rule. But alas, on his cruel command, he would systematically slaughter the male babes of Bethlehem in what would go down in history as one of the most dastardly atrocities known to man. Though the king be filled with such madness, it is unfathomable to imagine any good and decent soldier who would carry out the command and draw his sword against such innocence. To slay innocent children for the convenience of another is so sick. It is mind numbing to even try to picture the horror.

Of course, we try to comfort ourselves by distancing that time as an age of barbarianism, as an age where madness reigned. We now live in a more sophisticated time, a time where we value all human life as precious. A time where all men have equal rights, no matter their sex, age, color, religion or nationality. No, we do not live in a barbaric age of men ruled by fleshly appetites and primitive hedonism and immorality.

Or do we? Have we only become sophisticated in our barbarianism? Yet because abortion is legal, we have the modern equivalent of foot soldiers, that is, doctors, nurses, and medical staff that have no qualms in slaughtering babies for profit and "prestige". They are selling baby parts to the highest bidder!

We dress up in ties, white medical overcoats, hold PhD's and yet we butcher babies from their mother's womb! Our politicians, liberal news anchors, commentators, experts and priests of the new morality are seen on CNN and mainstream media supporting and encouraging the bloodshed. Yet all the talking head celebrities and political super stars who militantly advocate for abortion are in fact guilty of propagating the murder of the innocent! God will hold them all accountable! (I know this seems "judgmental" because, well, it is... but isn't it better to judge ourselves now then to have God judge us later? *"For if we would judge ourselves, we would not be judged." 1 Corinthians 11:31*

The massacre of precious babies is the drenched red background of the rights and privileges for the promiscuous. The modern hedonism, "whatever-feels-good-do-it-it's- your-right" society pre-empts all long traditional moral absolutes.

During the Roman Empire, the very hype and noise of a blood thirsty bread and circus crowd invigorated the wicked rulers to showcase the carnage by watching the innocent be devoured by lions as entertainment for the masses.

So now does our own society have a great indictment against this age... to our shame and condemnation. We are supposed to be a better, more "progressive" humanity than our barbaric past predecessors.

How is it that our mainstream culture has gone incessantly mad? How is it that our moral compass is so way off kilter and very few even take it to heart? How is it that our nation could even consider electing anyone that would endorse and legislate this barbaric, murderous practice of abortion?

The whole Democrat platform has spiraled down into the abyss. Many Republicans are teetering. We are indeed a very wayward people who have slipped into a bottomless pit of promiscuous filth and degradation.

As a nation, we show our true hearts by the leaders we bring to power. We spit in the face of God by choosing to side with a political platform that wishes to only increase the carnage and the preachers and priests stay silent lest they offend the sinners who contribute to their livelihood.

We have brazenly offered our children up to be sacrificed as we bow down to the golden idol of prosperity and materialism. We have chosen our pocketbooks over our moral obligations. Yet God is still holy and He still brings judgment on the wicked, though they seem unchecked in their unholy agendas.

Do not be disheartened by the proliferation of the evil in our times. Though it seems to be rampant and empowered by mass appeal, God is bringing judgment to the nations. His mercy is extended now but the wrath of God is coming. It is not the fluff of false prophets. God fearing men have always cried out to warn of the Lord's anger against injustice and perversion.

Just because we don't see judgment so quickly, we may mock God as weak or unconcerned but be assured, every unrepentant wicked deed and sexual perversion will be judged! Especially the bloodshed of the innocent. We offend God's very providential hand of mercy that has made this nation once great. But we have left our righteousness as a nation and plunged ourselves into the coming wrath of an Almighty God.

This is not some wanna-be prophet's bitter, bigoted take on a modern world of "love and tolerance". This is divine scripture and the Word of the Living God!

"THE WRATH OF GOD is being revealed from heaven against all the godlessness and wickedness of men who suppress the truth by their wickedness." Romans 1:18

"Put to death, therefore, the components of your earthly nature: sexual immorality, impurity, lust, evil desires, and greed, which is idolatry. Because of these, THE WRATH OF GOD is coming on the sons of disobedience." Colossians 3:5-6

"For of this you can be sure: No immoral, impure, or greedy person (that is, an idolater), has any inheritance in the kingdom of Christ and of God. Let no one deceive you with empty words, for because of such things GOD's WRATH comes on the sons of disobedience. Therefore do not be partakers with them." Ephesians 5:5-7

We have put in severe jeopardy this great Republic as the new liberal, socialist agenda slowly seeps into power. We have heard them cry for true change... and true change is coming! But not a change for the better but a change that will hasten an end to the great American experience, all of our Christian influence, freedoms and our constitutional rights. Our nation will not last long if we continue down the path of this violence, perversion and bloodshed! May God have mercy on all of us!

Our political leaders all speak to pamper the crowd with their promises to bring change, real hope and prosperity. Yet we are truly dead in the water before they even step to the podium.

How can "God bless America" if we are "godless America"?

The usual political message of a lawless, "liberal" political system is how they will be a true agent of change and redemption to the ills of our nation but in the end only make men applaud with monotony and distracted issues.

The truth is, it's not "about the economy, stupid". It's not about the endless wars. It's not about the housing crisis, the energy crisis, high taxes, terrorism or climate change. These are all outward symptoms of an inward cancer.

Throughout history you can see the rise and fall of nations and the one true thing that conquered all these empires.

Corruption from within brought about their demise from without. A moral and just nation will always rise with God's blessings. A decadent and unjust nation will eventually fall. Every political, societal or economic ill or major natural disaster a nation begins to experience is most assuredly tied directly to the cause and effect of sin in that nation. It is a fact that a nation that "forgets God", that forgets the principles of truth, justice and mercy will be "turned into hell"... so says the prophet of the Psalms. (Psalms 9:17)

God can only bless America when America is on the side of God, morality and truth. Now that we have strayed significantly away from Godly principles, God has become our enemy who now fights against us!

I genuinely weep for America and the visions I have seen of horrendous judgment yet to come on our dear Republic! This may seem to be far removed from the flatteries of polished preachers and an over positive generation. But mark my words, America's religious lukewarmness, hypocrisy, great sexual sins and the murder of millions of precious babies will not go unpunished! We should even now be waking up to the massive tragic events consistently unfolding across our nation. Massive fires and floods, pestilence, freak storms, civil unrest, an exponential increase in mass shootings, bloodshed and violence on our streets, these are all grievous signs of how the sins of this nation are bringing chaos and judgment.

Abortion may seem an insignificant issue but truly it is the greatest catalyst among many moral issues that are directly linked to the economic and military stability of our nation.

Of course, if our nation is to survive it will be more than just the reversal of abortion legislation that will have to take precedence in our courts and in our society. There are many moral issues being challenged today that if left unchecked will surely bring down the wrath of God on our beloved nation.

America has continued to be in moral free fall and rapid decay... or more aptly put, suicidal madness. America will soon be fighting for more than what moral dilemmas confront her. She will soon be fighting for her very existence on the world stage as a superpower, as the wealthiest nation, as the leader of the free world.

We are living in very desperate times and yet most of us are oblivious to what's really going on just below the surface of our culture, our government and the global, geopolitical changes alarmingly taking place even now. We are not "connecting the dots"!

We are still so distracted by trivial and vain pursuits. Whether the mainstream media or influential leaders continue to suppress the fact or not, the truth is, the Biblical prediction of "distress of nations" is here and now. The current global instabilities of world economies and military endeavors have moved the official "doomsday clock" up to almost midnight and we are just one mis-step away from World War III on so many fronts. We are not awake to the perilous end time signs that God's Word says must happen before He comes back.

Have you heard about the boiling frog experiment? It shows that if a frog is placed in boiling water, it will jump out immediately. However, a frog can be boiled alive if the water is heated very slowly. It becomes ever so slightly desensitized to the temperature rising. The frog will never jump out, oblivious to its own demise!

Incremental changes... ever so slightly makes for the best way to deceive and is the craftiest of ways to bring a people into real bondage. The devil takes more souls to fire lake on the "slow escalator to Hell" than any other vehicle!

We are so naïve if we believe that real evil does not secretly conspire all around us. Conspiracy has always been a fact of this corrupt humanity. Yes Virginia, conspiracy is everywhere and corruption is rampant in our governments, in our corporations, in our religious and educational institutions, in every facet of society and culture. Humanity is sick with self-centeredness and evil plotting.

Jesus was a conspiracy nut because He said all mankind was under the sway of the wicked one, groping in darkness and corruption. The scriptures bear out that all of mankind is wicked and sinful to the core without God as their center. The depravity of all men means that conspiracy and corruption is unimaginably prolific and deep rooted! Such ignorance and naivety makes us truly oblivious to any horrors and corruption brewing underneath the superficial glimmer and the facades of our dumbed down, distracted society. This is how the Nazi's swooped in and in just a few short decades totally deceived the German people.

So many Jews and the world for that matter were oblivious to the "final solution" and the gas chambers during WW2. It is because by nature most of us have a naive awareness that does not allow us to believe that men could be so cruel or that such evil intent could truly exist within the hearts of others. Christians can be the worst at such naivety. We don't want to see the world as dark and wicked. Ignorance is bliss. We want to always appear to others as "positive" and "encouraging" without a hint of discerning evil or making righteous lines in the sand. No instead, let's stick our heads in the sand and say "It ain't so".

Yet one of the most fundamental truths that Jesus repeatedly emphasized was "Let no man deceive you." Especially, as the "end of days" approaches. The admonition to watch and warn, to discern and not to be deceived is so overwhelmingly urged in the Holy Scriptures.

Deception is the enemy's greatest tool to enslave men. Discernment on the other hand, is only the friend of vigilant men who guard their freedom and the truth with fierceness. Yet where are the discerning men of this age? Where are the watchmen on the wall? Where are the true prophets who pierce the fluffy atmosphere of lying spirits with truth and righteousness? Where are the weeping Jeremiahs who warn to their own reputation and hurt that judgment is nigh and the "Babylonians are coming?"

We should make ourselves aware of the gradual societal changes that are happening now more than ever before and be confrontive and engaged. These changes are not only creating a great moral vacuum in our society but are taking us down a slippery slope of no return from the security and wealth that America has been so used to as a blessed nation. Our military might and monetary power is being challenged in so many ways today. As it appears to the discerning eye, those challenges will very soon increase exponentially.

The global tensions mounting especially in regards to China, Russia, and the Middle East and the economic trade wars (and war against the dollar as the "world currency") is indicative of the fragility of the times. We are on our way to suffering catastrophic, horrific loss both as American individuals and as a nation.

The solution is not merely outward political or economic policy reformation. It is mostly moral ambiguity that has us in such great peril. America is so polarized and divided in a frightful clash of culture and ideology which is due largely from this spiritual decay. We must become totally engaged in the social and spiritual warfare that now faces us. We are in a desperate hour and it is already too late to change some of the consequences of our reckless, debt based materialism and demoralized culture as a nation.

We are more concerned about our carpet matching our drapes, or whose winning on America's Got Talent and other vain, entertaining distractions than we are about the social, spiritual, moral and political decay of our times! What's it going to matter if we have a nice, updated kitchen if tomorrow our house burns to the ground? Am I saying we should never take care of trivial or vain issues in life... no, but neither should we be ever so consumed in things that have no earthly impact or eternal substance.

As Christians, we must be categorically different. No longer can we be lukewarm, nonchalant, apathetic, distracted or unconcerned. We must become radicalized in our faith and our activism.

This doesn't mean radical as in violent or terroristic. We are not talking about blowing up abortion clinics or killing abortion doctors. This is not what true Christians do. We don't fight wickedness with wickedness.

We can't love the sinner and ungodly by holding up a sour face as we hold up a picket sign yelling "Bloody Murderers"! Screaming and scowling at them only makes them more livid and loud in their own intentions. We must peaceably engage them in dialogue and respectful confrontation, to use Holy Spirit conviction and truth to persuade men of their sins. We can only use love, reason and common sense to hopefully change hearts and minds. Truth spoken in anger will set men off... Truth spoken in love will set men free.

We must talk and walk out moral transformation and getting back to love, truth and decency. Hypocrisy and politically correct dead religion must be thrown out of our churches. We must promote true love for God and for people. It is crucial to stay back the tide of filth and decadence. It's not just about changing the laws, changing political parties or changing the godless medias. The only way out of this morally deplete mess is in changing the hearts of the people! Without a great spiritual awakening, a metamorphosis of the hearts of the multitude, we are truly doomed as a nation! We must have a real revival and moral revolution if America is truly to survive as a free country. It is our enemies hope that we will spiral out of control into lawlessness and anarchy so that a new godless, dictatorial global order can be established in this present world.

Yes, we need to stop the killings, the bloodshed of the innocent. We need to save our children and then we may find mercy with the One who holds the nations in His hands. We can not stop the bloodshed until we realize and confess our own blood guiltiness, until our hearts and minds are vexed with conviction over the slaughter we have so carelessly allowed by our indifference, or worse, by our support of it. We must turn from our own sins and complacency. We must return to a passion for holiness and purity! Jesus can give us his nature, if we are willing to receive it.

Our apathy and distraction is no excuse to have turned a blind eye from protecting the innocent. It is time those of us who really are for truth, justice and mercy to band together and let our leaders know that we are still a present force to be reckoned with and a moral bulwark to hedge the flow of innocent blood. We must stand more bravely against the evil tide rising or I am afraid, we will be totally swept away by it.

The Empty Crib

Alas, If any woman could peer into the future and see the son or daughter she was aborting, she would never, never commit such an unmotherly, inhumane act against her own conscience, her own happiness or the beloved child that could have been!

Oh, when she doubts that she could ever be a "good mother" or is persuaded that she is unfit to hold such a title, she does not realize that all "good mothers" are born and develop just when their babies do!

A pregnancy terminated does not only kill a baby but also kills a mother... and might I add, a father too. When a mother chooses to take the life of her child, she chooses to die along with that child... to die a thousand deaths of happy parental moments that would have inspired and given purpose to her own existence.

She may emphatically affirm in a duped perspective, a "woman's right to privacy" or her "right to choose" but in so doing she denies the very essence of her womanhood. She shatters the delicate, God given motherly instincts within her very nature and purpose. She is not only aborting the precious son or daughter who clings within her for dear life... she is aborting a pathway of joyous motherhood and the spontaneous essence of new life and youthfulness.

The empty crib brings an empty life which hangs like a thick grey cloud of loneliness, shame and blood-guiltiness over the young women who do not acknowledge their dastardly deed or change their position and seek forgiveness on their decision to abort. With such guilt, you either reconcile your mind by true penance or by self justification.

Penance leads to forgiveness and healing but self justification leads to a deadening of the conscience, hardness of heart and madness of the mind. As we actually observe today seeing militant feminists go into full "zombie" defiance mode where they insolently celebrate the decision to kill their babies. Many human studies have shown that guilt not properly dealt with or suppressed brings on mental illness. This nation is full of blood guiltiness and subsequently, societal psychopathy.

Abortion is not a small implosion that collapses in its own little footprint just leaving a small gaping hole in the life of the mother. It is more like a nuclear bomb that can and will effect the lives of a whole family, even a whole society and culture. Yes, abortion destroys a baby and all the potential and destiny it would have had in the world... but did you ever stop to think how many others and their potentials are destroyed? Mothers, fathers, grandparents, brothers, sisters, uncles, aunts, nephews, nieces, cousins, etc.? The destruction of life leaves a vacuum, a void of potential love and laughter, joy and contentment in so many who may have benefited from such a life.

As a middle aged father myself, I can say that the new life of my children forced me to live young again, to think young, to be young.

A new life entrusted to one's care forges a new bond and a new destiny that makes your life exponentially take on real purpose and meaning. The only reason that abortion is even an ungodly reality is because too many people are miserably self centered to allow a baby to dynamically change their egocentric universe. They are, in essence people who have shriveled up from humanity's true calling, to our God given mandate to "love one another." Babies and children force us too stretch our characters in a very wonderful way. No longer are we self absorbed in our own little world. We are forced to learn to focus on another, one more helpless, more needy than ourselves. We grow in patience, in humility and in service to another. We learn to love, to care, to endure. We become human. Babies make us human again.

Oh but an ominous lamentation echoes within the heartstrings of a few noble men and women today. They are the most tender in their consciences among us who are transfixed in perpetual mourning for the brutal slaying of the countless unborn. Behind their black veils are the thousand tears of Rachel, weeping for her children, for they are not! They are not like so many of us who have deadened our consciences and trivialized the injustice of the killing of precious babies. The innocent blood of these little martyrs cry out from the ground but we are too deaf to hear them, too deaf from the pursuit of our own happiness. We are willfully distracted by our shopping mall sales and by our favorite sport's team.

We force our thoughts to think on the shallow, the superficial appetites and the blatant materialism we are so fond of. Let's not pain our mind and heart with negative things and horrific realities around us. Let us not think on those precious little ones whose blood is spilled every day, like little lambs to the slaughter. To the gods of our narcissistic and hedonistic culture, we salute.

This book, "Angels In The Snow" was not written for your leisurely entertainment. It was not written to be a quaint little story that you get warm fuzzies from and then put it on a shelf to soon forget. It is for your great awakening! It is for your righteous indignation! It is for your passionate calling as a human being with a God given conscience to stand for the truth that is too evident to ignore! It is written to slap in the face, the insidious perspectives of a hedonistic, self serving generation. It is written in hopes to rekindle a dying ember of decent, wholesome influence in a society gone mad, in moral mayhem.

Oh, but how long will the wicked reign?

Yes, I hope to shake the sleepy-eyed, morally vexed among us, back to our conscientious obligation to defend the innocent and fight for the causes of justice and truth. I pray for radical reform, righteous rage and real revival!

This writer hides behind no respectable status quo of compromise or tries to veneer my true intentions. If the full force of my motives for this story were completely made into a reality, all intentional, man induced abortions would be outlawed as murder in the first degree! Yes, I am aware that such statements seem so "oppressively puritanical" or arbitrarily close-minded to certain "situational ethics." However, to those of us who fear God, we do not have the liberty to amend or add clauses to one of the Ten Commandments. Murder is murder and killing a baby for any reason is murder. There is no justification or "scenario" where we should play God. Just as if a woman and a baby were in a car wreck and a good doctor had to choose... he would first try to save both lives but then concentrate on the one he surmised as prospectively in more urgent need of care or chance of success. He would not intentionally kill one of them for any reason. If the neglected one in that moment died, then the doctor would be guiltless as he did all he could humanely do. These "crisis pregnancy situations" are in fact so rare that they should not even be mentioned as some sort of argument or justification for abortion.

This is not radical or "oppressive". It may seem radical but only because we have become so far removed from the fundamentals of decency, morality and justice. "Radical" today is what was regular and normal just a few short years ago... when we knew God's Word through and through.

Now that the wicked reign and the heathen rage in this modern world, the voice of conscience and reason can hardly be heard. The left leaning medias, be it the mainstream controlled news or the entertainment industry are so morally bankrupt that they are constantly pushing propaganda to make the good guys look like bad guys, right looks wrong and wrong appears right. It is deceptively done in the name of "freedom" from the shackles of our traditional, puritanical, Christian heritage.

But isn't it ironically confusing to have the audacity to say that "protecting and saving the lives of precious babies is oppressive to women" while allowing their wholesale slaughter and marketing their body parts to the highest research bid is not "oppressive at all" but instead "progressive"? Tell me, what crazy world did these people come from and why aren't these whacked out politicians in straight jackets?

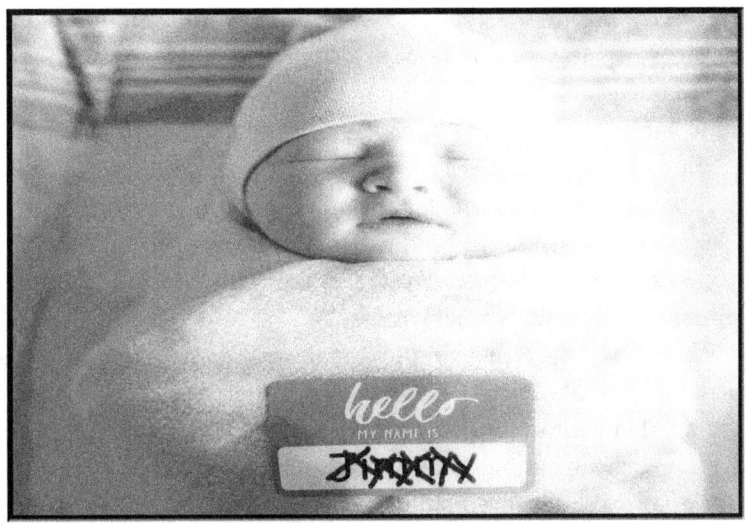

I Didn't Do Enough

So why have many of us become so ho-hum apathetic about the sacrificing of our nation's children on the altar of demon gods? Why is it that we can clink champagne glasses and think America is great again just because we have a little more wad of filthy money in our bank accounts?

I have always been fascinated about the German people during World War II. How they could go about their lives as if things were usual, laughing, dancing and doing business when just on the other side of the train tracks the chimney stacks pumped out putrid smoke from the burning corpses of a million Jews. How could a whole society be so brainwashed, so dead in their consciences to the horrors and the injustices? How could anyone with any moral fortitude not risk their own comfort and convenience to speak out in revolutionary protest over the atrocities happening around them? But I looked no further than my own heart to find the answers.

You see, abundance, materialism, prosperity and wealth always breeds a self absorbed culture. A society more concerned about their sporting events, their fashionable looks, their bottom dollar profits and of course, most importantly, to blend in with the "cool", the "elite" the "status quo".

Heaven forbid we appear to be radical and extreme about any of our views lest we stand out like a sore thumb and rain on the popular parades around us... Lest our Christianity makes others feel uncomfortable.

Thus we are not about to rock the boat and speak so radically against abortion or for that matter any other immoral issue of our day. We water down the message to a nice lukewarm temperature so that everyone can feel comfortable around us... or at least lukewarm too. Happiness and joy joy... at what cost?

We are too concerned about reputation and respect. So we live in a generation that fears to stand alone or appears to be on the fringes. We are apathetic and part of a pathetic cookie cutter generation of mainstream fish swimming towards the flushing noise.

We are "well balanced souls" that must remain polite, passive and dignified when our children are horrendously butchered and decapitated and our woman raped of their virtue and honor by way of militant hedonism and feminism.

The spirit of wicked Jezebel now permeates the land. Where is the spirit of holy Elijah to confront her? Yes, women have been oppressed and it's awesome to see a lot of that changing. I love that women are able to succeed in business and pursue many things that are were once only traditionally men-related. However, militant feminism that makes women hate or despise men or arrogantly compete against men is the devil's extreme. Especially the feminism that laughs impudently at God and man and shouts "I'm proud to have killed my baby!"

Yet the spirit of Elijah needs to rebuke the spirit of Jezebel even if it makes a lot of seduced, neutered eunuch, "church leaders" get dizzy from their spiritual stupor.

The "fear of man is a snare" and we are all captured by it to remain passive and pampered.

But who is that wild man, that prophet crying in the wilderness, that whistle-blower, that fanatic no one feels comfortable around? He is the one who fears not men but God alone, who dares to speak to convict men of their shame. He is the one who shall be ostracized, blackballed and ridiculed for his "outspoken views" and so called "radical ideas". But only because of our corporate silence and apathy does one who stands alone seem outspoken or passionately radical.

One may seem radical when in fact he is only being normal in a subnormal culture. A man may look like a raving madman to a sleepy eyed people but in a burning house his shouts of "Fire! Fire!" should not be dismissed as fringe fanaticism. No, he is a valiant man of honor trying to save his fellow from the flames!

Are we really guiltless if we sit idly by and silently know that millions of babies are being slaughtered all around us?

I hear people say that we shouldn't be "insensitive" to the troubled teens and single mothers who are the majority that end up getting these abortions. We should tread lightly here. Speak softly without offending anyone... You know, not so intense or urgently passionate or forthright in defining it as "evil" or murderous.

Yet these precious babies are poisoned, suffocated, burned, ripped from limb to limb, their heads decapitated, their skulls crushed and brains sucked out in a brutal, painful, violent way!

But we should use the soft terminology to describe these violent practices? We should be more loving in our presentation of these truths?

But truth is compromised by watering it down to substitute goobily gook terminology that does not reflect the brutal violence truly taking place.

That is why we are where we are today!

It's time those girls know that it is a precious baby that they are killing! It is time that they know that it is not just a mass of fetal tissue! It is not a parasite or cancer in their uterus. It is a baby... a beautiful, precious baby!

Yes, of course, we should be merciful and tender towards those girls and women who are broken for their past choice of abortion and need to know that God can forgive them. Mercy is always the first response to brokenness and humility. Yet to the proud, impudent, militant, Pro-choice advocates who seethe with the blood of the unborn, we warn them to flee from the wrath to come! Mercy to the humble. Judgment to the proud. It's always been God's way. Jesus always granted mercy to the broken but declared judgment on the proud.

Others say we shouldn't make women, doctors, nurses, lawyers and politicians accountable to what abortion really is... murder. We shouldn't make them ashamed for killing babies? We have become a people that brazenly do wickedly with no shamefacedness! Contrary to popular political correctness, shame and guilt are not "bully" emotions to our psyches to make us feel sad and bad and suicidal... but more like coaches and drill sergeants to get us to recognize moral failure, sins, perversions, faults and erroneous thinking to motivate us to change and do what is good, moral, decent and right! If we don't feel shame or guilt for our sins or shortcomings, we will never change to be a better person.

Like the unbelievable, absurd tragedy of the Wal-Mart employee, trampled to death by a crowd of self absorbed zombies who wanted to save a few bucks on a toaster oven on Black Friday. The man cried out for someone to help him. Instead, a glazed over, greedy crowd plowed right over his body, crushing the life breath out of him. It was reported that when shoppers were notified that the man had died, some of the crowd trying to justify themselves belligerently shouted "I waited in line all night!" Have we really gotten to such a place in our society where shame and guilt are replaced with insolent pride and self justification?

Are we really that sick? What kind of humanity have we nurtured by our hedonistic, "I-want-it-now, I-deserve-it-now" culture? I deeply shudder knowing our society is truly going mad with no moral compass! Where are the persons who pull away from the madness to help a fallen brother to get back up? Where are those who will shame and convict the morally deplete crowd even to their own hurt? Where are those who will boldly proclaim that abortion is truly murder and those who support it or assist in the practice of it, will one day be held accountable as murderers to the righteous Judge of all the earth, to the true "supreme court" of Heaven?

You say that "murder" is way too strong of a word. We shouldn't be that radical or blunt. Really?

Why do we readily convict murderers of small children or babies and shame them as the greatest of all sick criminals? Because it is in our hearts as a God given sense of justice to shame and punish those who prey on the innocent and defenseless. We all cry out from our very being to bring swift and severe justice to those who harm one of these little ones! Why are we not pleading for the cause of these precious unborn like that?

Why are we so apathetic and distracted by the vain and trivial?

In a powerful, dramatic moment within the movie Schindler's List, Schindler, even though credited as saving many Jews from the Nazi atrocities, reflects out loud to his own shame, how many more Jews he could have saved if only he had not been distracted by vanities and given up more of his material wealth-

Oskar Schindler: I could have got more out. I could have got more. I don't know. If I'd just... I could have got more.

Itzhak Stern: Oskar, there are eleven hundred people who are alive because of you. Look at them.

Oskar Schindler: If I'd made more money... I threw away so much money. You have no idea. If I'd just...

Itzhak Stern: There will be generations because of what you did.

Oskar Schindler: I didn't do enough!

Itzhak Stern: You did so much. [Schindler looks at his car]

Oskar Schindler: This car. Goeth would have bought this car. Why did I keep the car? Ten people right there. Ten people. Ten more people.

[removing Nazi pin from lapel]

Oskar Schindler: This pin. Two people. This is gold. Two more people. He would have given me two for it, at least one. One more person. A person, Stern. For this. [sobbing] I could have gotten one more person... and I didn't! And I... I didn't!

~Schindler's List

As in the movie, I think of the wasted time and energy that we American Christians do on so much trivial and vain things. How much we obsess over our extravagant and fluffy lifestyles. How we stress out over the smallest losses and truly insignificant troubles. We have become so spoiled with our society of instant gratification. We have become a culture that has built every invention to make us lazy and unthinking. When it comes to the causes and the crusades we willingly follow, it is only those that will benefit our selfish agendas that we end up pimping out for. If it brings controversy or costs us something, forget it. We don't want to be part of anything where it is not popular, fashionable or lucrative. We think that if the "sheeple" of the world look down on it, it must be bad or uncool.

So we constantly schedule our emptiness and vanity to keep us surrounded by the superficial. We will not sacrifice for a worthy cause, especially one as politically explosive as abortion. We pat ourselves on the back for our neutral, lukewarm position- "Yes, we are not so radical like those other extreme Christians." We ride the fence of compromise with no shame or guilt.

But one day, will we not blush at our indifference? Will we not like Oskar Schindler, wonder why we were so nonchalant and pathetically distracted by our petty lifestyles?

What if I had stood up to that liberal teacher in the classroom? What if I had not gone along with my peers? What if I had voted for the politician that was unpopular and blasted by a liberal fake news media? What if I had pleaded with that girl to keep her baby? What if I had boycotted that business that helped fund the killing of babies? What if I had stood alone? What if I had honored God and not men?

Where are those who do not follow the crowd? Where are those who fight for the truth no matter the cost?

I am afraid that we do not possess the fortitude and strength of character as our forefathers who built this nation with sweat, tears and true morale. We are apathetic about truth, justice and mercy. We suckle at the teats of a great propaganda media machine on the television, radio, print and internet. We have become mindless sheeple who allow those medias to think for us and to mold our minds to become "non character players" where we go along to get along with the mainstream "consensus". We all react the same when we hear someone cry "foul!" We assume they are all nut jobs and any naysayer or dissenter is a socially underdeveloped individual. Yet could the herd of sheeple people be a controlled group, designed for the slaughter? Could we who are so proud to be "free thinkers" be truly a product of social engineering and brainwashing?

Think outside the box... the box being the one with the remote control! In a world full of corruption and deception, why don't we question everything... instead of nothing?

Our Holy Creator will not allow the bloodshed to continue indefinitely. He will send swift and severe judgment on our nation, America and this present world. I can stress this enough. This may seem out of step with the "happy prosperity and bless me, bless me" churches and ministries but God is not mocked people! He is holy and just.

I too could do as I have done before and turn a blind eye to the issue of abortion. I could stay silent. I could stop writing, stop posting on social media.

But as one born out of such circumstances, I feel a sense of duty, a sense of obligation, a sense of purpose. I am haunted as I hear my unborn brothers and sisters crying for a chance to live as I now do. I hear them pleading with my conscience to do something, anything to save some of them, if I can.

Oh, I may not go down as any great reformer or leader. My future gravestone will probably go unnoticed... but that's very okay. I don't really care for corrupted accolades or endorsements by mere mortal, fallen men. We are all as worms before this great and mighty, eternal God.

But when I stand before my Creator and He asks me, what did I do to help stem the flood of wickedness? What did I do to help save the sheep from the slaughter? What did I do to turn souls back to truth, justice and mercy? What did I do to turn the hearts of men towards God?

I do not want to stand ashamed, with only the dust of things to offer up. My car, my house, my big screen TV, my gold and silver, my great employments, my lands, my social network following, my petty self serving causes, my wasted life... all dust and vapor, forgotten vanities in eternity!

I want to say to my God, "I fought for you, Lord. I fought for innocence. I fought for those who were defenseless. I fought for truth, justice and mercy. I may not have won as the world sees victory. I may have stood alone and perhaps even to be martyred... but I fought for you Jesus!"

I want my Lord to say to me, "You indeed fought and were faithful. Enter into the joy of your Lord!"

But even then, glory and shame will kiss each other for a moment in eternity. Then I will meet my brothers and sisters who were the little unborn martyrs of my generation. They will all come up to me and hug me for trying, trying to save some of them. And then I will weep on the shoulders of those who died while I stayed silent, those who were stolen from humanity's bosom while I pursued my petty vanities. I will not look them in the eye but then they will lift my head and wipe my tears. They will forgive me and we will both forget that shame and bloodshed ever came between us.

I do not know how this story, "Angels In the Snow" will be received. Or these subsequent messages I have poured out in tears and trembling. We live in a mixed up generation filled with every sort of mixed up "perspective" in the world. But even if one life is affected by it, if one unborn baby is saved by it, then it will have served it's purpose. There will be one less tear I will have to shed in heaven. I pray for the day when there are no tears on earth! I pray for the day when there are no tears in heaven!

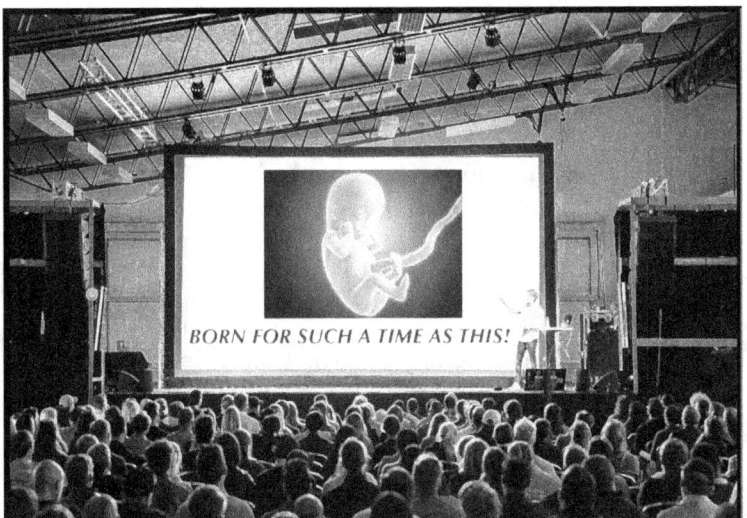

Born For Such A Time As This

In conclusion, I know that I have spoken much about our shame, our sin and judgment in regards to abortion. I also know that such ideas do not sit well with a generation of ear tickled people whose spiritual instruction has mostly been a candy coated, feel good, "bless-me, bless me" kind of Churchianity. We do not like our consciences sliced and diced with truth. We have become a super sensitive people who cringe to hear any context of judgment or negativism in a message. The false prophets cry "peace, prosperity and safety and the people love it so." But has God become a fluffy bunny rabbit who no longer becomes wrathful against injustice and evil? No, it is we who have become fluffy. However, such truthful medicine may taste bad or give a sort of knee jerk reaction to we, who've been spoiled by flatteries... but if we will allow its healing properties to be assimilated into our consciences, we will awake more humane and godly.

I also know that "mercy triumphs over judgment." I know that if a people repent of their sins, God relents of His judgment. Even God's warning of judgment is so that He can show mercy in the end. If God were as sadistic as many paint Him out to be, He would not even send a warning. There would be no need for prophets. He would just send fire and annihilate us. But our Father God is not like that at all. No, He is not a shriveled up, bitter old divine being who has lightening bolts in one hand and a law book in the other. Yet neither is He a "fluffy teddy bear" God who when you hug him, He only gives you warm fuzzies and says syrupy "I love you's."

Like a beautiful diamond, He is a multi-faceted God of holiness and love. *"Behold the goodness and severity of God!" Romans 11:22* He reluctantly holds judgment in one hand against the unrepentant but eagerly holds mercy in the other for those who are broken over their sins.

Jonah knew God's true dispositional leaning is always towards mercy. This is why he didn't want to warn the people of Nineveh. He would look like a liar and a false prophet if the people repented and God relented. A whale of a time later, Jonah finally obeyed and warned of the judgment to come. Sure enough, the people cried out for mercy and changed their hearts. The mercy of God followed and Jonah's prophesy became null and void for that generation, that moment of time.

Many of us also have been burned by wild eyed, whacked out, wanna-be prophets whose message of judgment was perhaps right in word but not in spirit. In my youth, I was a victim of a brute gospel that seemed to bully people into serving God through fear. It emphasized damnation more than salvation, Hell and God's wrath more than hope and mercy.

Jesus rebuked James and John for wanting to call down fiery judgment from heaven on a people. His rebuke was that "they knew not what manner of spirit they were of." Today, we have many "sons of thunder" whose judgment message is lacking the prime ingredient to God's true heart- mercy. True prophets are weeping prophets more than whipping prophets. They warn with tears and trembling. They warn with meekness and gentleness. They speak judgment with mercy in mind. May God send us men who will be bold enough to speak the truth but humble enough to speak it in a spirit of love and mercy.

I know the Father will show mercy to all who are broken and contrite over the slaughter of innocence. "The measure of God's mercy goes far beyond the measure of our sins."

Now, for all of you girls and young women who were lied to by a social worker, doctor or counselor and you gave up your baby to those murderers, you can be forgiven by God! He will not only forgive you but He will arrange it so that your sons and daughters will one day meet you on that heavenly shore. They will kiss your face and escort you into paradise to the Father's eternal care!

For all of you social workers and counselors who now see the error of your ways... you too can be forgiven! You were deceived by a bloody culture gone mad when you whispered "murder, murder" as the way to comfort a distraught or encumbered mother. But God sees your regretful sorrow. He sees your tongue has changed. He now whispers "life, life" to your own mortal frame.

For all of you doctors whose profession was to be a healer, a life-giver and caretaker but you betrayed your Hippocratic Oath and slew the precious children you were mandated to protect. You chose to kill them for your own financial gain and career advancement. But now you drop your instruments of death and try to vigorously scrub the blood off your hands. Your guilt is so deep and you weep with such regret! Lift up your eyes, oh son of humanity, God has seen your tears! Physician, heal thyself with God's mercy... you are forgiven... go and sin no more!

For all of you lobbyists, lawyers, judges and political leaders who have spurned your own conscience to bring about laws of lawlessness, supporting the murder of the innocent. You who have helped legalize the slaughter of precious unborn souls. You have entitled and empowered a generation to kill their beautiful sons and daughters... But now you throw down your picket signs and burn your campaign posters in an attempt to distance yourself from the evil you once created. You now wake up in the middle of the night poised with your hands against a phantom tide to stem the flow of the blood you once encouraged. Your repentant tears have fallen upward and God has stamped "FORGIVEN" over your name!

All of us, especially church leaders who have remained complacent, compromised, distracted and apathetic about the infanticide and the "two doors down holocaust"... who would rather splurge a thousand dollars on a one night sports extravaganza then to donate a few bucks to a Christian crisis pregnancy center... who idly sit by and say not a word as militant advocates spew their vile philosophies at us and at our children. We too can find redemption from our compromise and fear of man! We can be forgiven for our lack of conviction and moral outrage.

Yes, I guess I am trying to get under your skin. Even though we may not directly be responsible for the horrific slaughter of babies, we need not get cozy and comfy as our society slowly boils away our moral foundations. We need to jump out of the pan of water and warn our fellow man of the dangers of a world without moral absolutes and the slippery slope of *"every man doing what seems right in his own eyes."*

Lastly, I plead with you, dear reader. Do not digest this story and these after thoughts without careful reflection on what part you may play today in saving the lives of many dear children! The smallest pebble can make everlasting ripples! "What we do here and now will echo in eternity." Never sell yourself short on what you can do as one mere man. "We may be just one in this world but we can be the world to just one." With God all things are possible! The world has seen in the past what one mighty heart can stir up!

We all have a purpose. Dive heart first in a cause greater than yourself. Make your life count for something other than solely chasing the "American dream." What is the "American dream" without the great American heritage of truth, justice and mercy? Make your life count for eternity.

We need to really pray. Pray for the hearts of men to change. Pray for a metamorphosis in the moral disposition of our leaders and our society, especially in our churches!

I am no one really... to speak on these matters. I am only obeying my God and my conscience as I discern the evil times, the end times. But I am a "brand plucked out of the fire." And I need to try to pluck others from the fire as well. I know I can make a difference. Therefore I will do what I can.

Remember the story of the starfish thrower.

The story goes that a young girl was walking along a beach where thousands upon thousands of starfish had been washed up during a terrible storm. When she came to each starfish, she would pick it up, and throw it back into the ocean. People watched her with amusement.

She had been doing this for quite some time when a man approached her and said, "Little girl, why are you doing this? Look at this beach! You can't save all these starfish. You can't even begin to make a difference!"

The girl was crushed and suddenly deflated. But after a few moments, she again bent down, picked up another starfish, and hurled it as far as she could into the ocean. Then she looked up at the man and replied,

"Well, I made a difference to that one!"

The old man looked at the girl and thought about what she had done and said. Inspired, he joined the little girl in throwing starfish back into the sea. Soon others joined in, and before you know it, all the starfish were saved that day.

We have something more precious than starfish to save.

Whether you are just an individual, or church or ministry, it is all of our calling to stand against abortion. You may say that your calling is to feed the hungry and give shelter to the homeless... but guess what? God made us able to do multi-tasking. We can walk and chew gum at the same time. We can be called to all things Godly and all things needful. Don't make the mistake of neglecting a thousand opportunities to do good, in pursuit of a simple or singular mission. You can be Pro-Life and serve widows and orphans too. Don't limit yourself in doing good. Of course, be led by His Spirit but I think the Spirit leads us to fight on all fronts against evil.

Don't worry about how others perceive you as "being political" for in the end, we all are, really. Whether it is by our voice or by our silence, by our passion or by our complacency, by our knowledge and understanding or by our ignorance and apathy, we all show our real alliances and what kingdom we truly stand for. Hopefully, you are on the winning side. My bet and vote is on the one, true and living God.

So in conclusion, I pray "Angels In The Snow" both the story and the heartfelt messages afterwards have caused all of us to do some real soul searching. I pray that many would take these weeping words of burden I have shared to heart. I pray that we would perhaps lay prostrate alone before the Lord God Almighty and weep for our own lack of love and passion for purity, truth and justice... and to intercede for these little ones being led as lambs to the slaughter.

Again, let us examine our hearts and not be a part of this last day, wicked generation whose love has grown cold. *"And because lawlessness will be increased, the love of many will grow cold."* **Matthew 24:12**

Let us not be desensitized and demoralized by the rampant sin to allow our hearts to grow indifferent to the injustices and suffering around us. Let us not live in "selfie mode" and only wish for other people to pay attention to us and our own surmised needs. We must through God's Spirit, find basic empathy, love and compassion for others. We urgently need to look beyond the veil of self existence and self survival. There is a whole world in desperate need of good people to demonstrate God's love and holiness with true selflessness. We have but one life to give to God and His purposes.

I pray that all of us would get up from our time with God with a renewed sense of purpose and destiny in living out authentic faith with conviction and precise directives to be both salt and light in a bland, tasteless, dark and dying world.

Let us pray for mercy on America and all the nations that are under judgment, set to perish because of their wickedness. Let us pray for mercy to stop the bloodshed of all the innocent, precious unborn babies being slaughtered today... that relief and deliverance may be our cause. Let us also pray for mercy on all of us who have been born to this world, into this last, perverse and adulterous generation... to stand up, stand out and stand together... to not remain silent... to somehow a make a difference... for God knows we were born for "such a time as this."

"For if you remain completely silent at this time, relief and deliverance will arise for the Jews from another place, but you and your father's house will perish. Yet who knows whether you have come to the kingdom for such a time as this?"
Esther 4:14

122

About The Author

Heath Christopher Goodman (1967 - ∞) (because he's gonna live forever) was born in Ft Wayne Indiana with birth defects to a few of his fingers, in other words, one of a kind, designer hands. Before that, he survived an attempted abortion. Death has tried to take him out many times since then. However, by God's grace and purposes, he still lingers in this fallen world for only God knows how much longer. He has a passion to give his testimony and promote all of his book's messages. He is a speaker, writer, and business owner. He is a licensed and ordained minister of the gospel, first and foremost by the calling of the Lord Jesus and by the Word of God.

Heath was licensed to preach by his second church, Milton Avenue Baptist Church, Brownwood Texas in 1985 at the age of 18 and ordained by the Missionary Methodist Church while attending Youth With A Mission in the late 1990's. He has labored with several ministries through the years such as Keith Green's Last Days, YWAM, and Calvary Commission doing missionary work and evangelism. He is available to give his testimony, speak passionately on the abortion issue or to preach the whole counsel of God in a spirit of love and mercy. He resides in a suburb of Atlanta, Georgia with his wife, Marivania, his daughter Jordanna and son Joshua.

He can be contacted directly by email at;
heathcgoodman@gmail.com

LEAVE YOUR MARK ON THE WORLD.
GET YOUR BOOK PUBLISHED TODAY!

Do you have a book inside you? Of course you do!

Everyone of us has a testimony or a story. Everyone of us has a lesson learned that could be turned into a story or teaching moment.

We need Christian authors who want to inspire and touch the lives of others through their Christian writing. There is such a void in this world for God-fearing, morality based stories for our children and for adults. We need you to help raise up the standard of truth and purity before the Lord!

Whether it is fiction or nonfiction, a children's book or for all of us big kids, we want to help you edit, illustrate and publish or "self publish" your God inspired, "heart-of-fire" literary masterpiece! Contact us now!

Get your book formatted, cover illustrated and printed within as little as a few weeks for a great price! You can utilize our pre-release Christian publishing service for anyone who wishes to get their draft book or manuscript printed as a book with a full color cover illustration. The pre release edition of your book can be used as a way to generate interest, serve as a "feedback release copy", give as gifts and even to submit it to other larger publishers as a concept release manuscript.

Or we can help you fully publish your book under our own publishing company, Creative Works Press. We do it all- from book formatting to cover design to acquiring ISBN numbers to printing copies to putting your book online in any format to reach millions of people and bookstores!

We do not retain any rights or royalties over your work. We can do a turn key service of designing, editing, formatting, printing and shipping a set number of copies to you. You market and sell your books however you wish. ISBN services and a website for your book are also available.

Creative Works Press is dedicated to being a high quality Christian publisher and bringing material that promote God honoring, beautiful, uplifting messages to it's readers. Like any publisher, we reserve the right to publish only material that identifies with our Christian mission statement and core values. Contact us today for a free consultation!

Creative Works Press
2001 Duncan Dr. NW Ste. #44
Kennesaw, GA 30156
404-307-9185
sales@creatorgraphics.com
www.CreativeWorks.cloud

CREATIVE WORKS PRESS

Leave Your Mark On The World.

Yes. We are dreaming big and praying earnestly. Why not?
We have a movie script and we're not afraid to use it!

Those who have read the story agree that it would make a great movie to truly help save precious babies and help the Pro-Life cause. Hollywood knows the power of entertainment and how it does more than "just entertain" but helps to shift people's minds and hearts towards intellectual, spiritual and social agendas. Why can't we do that?

COMING SOON?

Turning "Angels In The Snow" into a movie would not only bring a fresh awareness of the abortion issue to the forefront of the headline media but also would challenge many people to rethink their Pro-Choice position.

There are not many movies out there that actually confront the issue of abortion with a dramatic yet heartwarming story. A heartwarming Christmas story with a powerful message that could cause a fire to ignite the passion of hundreds of thousands to get involved with saving precious babies! Wouldn't that be more than awesome?

"Angels In The Snow" as a movie could reach untold millions in the screen fiend generation who don't like to read books, especially ones with a provocative and powerful message. It just might turn the hearts of mothers back to their babies, the hearts of fathers back to their children!

Heath has already produced a matching movie script and other media resources to bring to potential Christian movie producers, celebrities, politicians that could be instrumental in seeing the story com to the big screen.

If a fire was created in you by this book, or it blessed you in any way, we ask you to pray about helping us dream big, helping us see the story turned into a movie. Please go to http://AngelsInTheSnow.net to find out how you can truly help us by getting involved by donating some of your time, resources or finances to the Angel In The Snow Movie Project. While you're at the website, please be sure to click on the "Book Reviews" link to leave a review/comment about the book. We'd love to get your feedback!